DANCE OF TERROR

DANCE OF TERROR

Jean Morrant

CHIVERS
THORNDIKE

This Large Print book is published by BBC Audiobooks Ltd, Bath, England and by Thorndike Press®, Waterville, Maine, USA.

Published in 2006 in the U.K. by arrangement with the Author.

Published in 2005 in the U.S. by arrangement with Jean Hall.

U.K. Hardcover ISBN 1–4056–3446–4 (Chivers Large Print)
U.S. Softcover   ISBN 0–7862–8014–X (British Favorites)

The text of this Large Print edition is unabridged.
Other aspects of the book may vary from the original edition.

Set in 16 pt. New Times Roman.

Printed in Great Britain on acid-free paper.

British Library Cataloguing in Publication Data available

Library of Congress Cataloging-in-Publication Data

Morrant, Jean.
    Dance of terror / by Jean Morrant.
       p.   cm.
    "Thorndike Press large print British favorites."—T.p. verso.
    ISBN 0–7862–8014–X (lg. print : sc : alk. paper)
    1. Spain—Fiction. 2. Large type books. I. Title.
    PR6113.O755D36 2005
    823'.92—dc22
                                   2005017479

CHAPTER 1

'You will have to hurry, sir,' the clerk at the airport check-in advised. 'They're boarding now.'

Rafel nodded and headed towards the passport control, his hand sliding in to the pocket of his well-tailored suit as he moved forward, his long stride covering the distance in rapid time.

In the departure area the young lady who was waiting to exchange his ticket looked up, quickly replacing her expression of impatience with a welcome smile as she informed the handsome passenger, 'I am sorry, sir, only centre seats in First Class. Final call went out a few moments ago.'

Taking his boarding pass from her red-tipped fingers, he smiled and moved in to the waiting plane. Thankful to be on board he seated himself and, once settled, closed his eyes, allowing the sound of the powerful engines to drift through his mind as they prepared for take-off. He thought of the beautiful, old rosewood guitar which he had successfully bid for in auction earlier that afternoon, sensed the feel of its polished curves beneath his appreciative fingers and his lips slanted in silent pleasure. To have acquired such a classic item more than

1

compensated for the time it had taken for it to be properly packed and insured and the hair-raising taxi ride through London's busy streets in the subsequent panic to reach the airport.

Opening his eyes as the plane levelled out on its course, he cast a casual glance over the passengers nearby, coming to rest on the young woman seated by the window. He looked away, then back again to observe her more closely. By strange coincidence, she was the one who had bid against him in the saleroom only hours before! He recognised the same petite figure dressed in blue, carrying a curious handbag with a gilt handle, like a small executive case. He couldn't possibly be mistaken.

Frowning thoughtfully, he recalled her expression of despair when the auctioneer's gavel had come down in his favour. He clearly remembered seeing the anguish on her face before she had dropped her head to conceal her distress, her hair falling forward like a gleaming curtain of pale gold. When she had left the saleroom he'd felt a strong urge to go after her, explain that this particular instrument had belonged to his old tutor and was of great sentimental value. He wanted to assure her he would cherish an object of such unmistakable quality.

With a faint sigh he reclined his seat. It was quite ridiculous to concern himself like this. Most probably it had been merely a feminine whim, a desire to possess something antique with scant regard for its history, and she had left in a fit of pique. But the memory of her expression continued to trouble him. He couldn't dismiss it from his mind.

Suddenly, sensing her gaze upon him, he turned and saw that she was quite beautiful, her violet eyes veiled by long, thick lashes. Then, as if struck by recognition, her lips parted slightly and she swiftly averted her gaze. Perplexed, he ran his fingers through his crisp, dark hair, regretting the seat between them was occupied. He had to think of a way to open conversation, perhaps suggest a drink at Barcelona airport.

After the in-flight meal, he watched whilst she selected perfume from the duty-free trolley, preparing to catch her attention as the man seated between them reclined his seat. He saw her make room for her purchase in the small case when, hopeful of gaining a clue to her identity, he leaned across to peer down on the typewritten sheets it held.

Suddenly, his eyes were riveted to the paper and he stifled a sharp intake of breath. There, on a printed list, was his own name, Professor Rafel G Pujol, Barcelona, followed by his letters of distinction and learning, correct in every detail. He took a second glance before she brought down the lid to convince himself his vision was not playing tricks, and he ached from tension as his confused mind groped for a logical reason. Why did this stranger have his name on a list in her case? Should he question her now, or first engage her in conversation to discover her name and objective?

It was uncanny, yet there could be a perfectly simple explanation, one they could laugh over during a drink at the airport. He caught her looking in his direction and smiled, but she coolly ignored him and returned to face the small window, the sunlight dancing through her hair. Perhaps she didn't recognise him after all.

With mounting dismay he realised time was running out as the signal came to fasten seat-belts. After touchdown at Barcelona airport, he stood back to allow her to pass, but his neighbour did likewise, blocking the aisle, leaving her free to proceed towards the exit.

She remained well ahead all the way into the terminal building, but once inside he gained ground, edging forward in the queue for passport control until only one person stood between them. Eager to learn her name he leaned closer, straining his eyes to read her passport. 'Fiona Max . . .' he read then, couldn't catch any more.

Suddenly, as the pressure of the crowd built up behind him, he felt a sharp stab of pain in his thigh. Uttering a gasp of protest he swung round to glare at those close behind, but no-one apologised or appeared even slightly aware of his discomfort. And the uniformed

4

official shot him an impatient look as he waited to examine his passport.

Once through the barrier, he saw the girl standing beside the luggage carousel and slowed, deciding on the most tactful approach. Pausing a moment as a strange sensation overcame him, he ran his tongue over his lips and blinked to clear his vision. The heat was becoming intolerable. He eased a finger round the inside of his collar as beads of perspiration began to form on his brow, and advanced towards her with a curious feeling that his feet weren't touching the ground.

Her outline seemed to lose its clarity as he lurched forward. Sounds faded and returned and his limbs trembled uncontrollably as he endeavoured to fight the rising waves of nausea. Then he swayed, brushing against her as he fell into unconsciousness . . .

*   *   *

For a moment, Fiona thought the man she had seen at the saleroom in London had been about to speak to her then, quite unexpectedly, his legs buckled beneath him and he was lying at her feet on the polished marble floor. Immediately, she reached for his pulse then turned him on to his side and looked up to catch someone's attention. She had trained as a nurse so she was not given to panicking, but how was she to call for assistance when she spoke so little of the language?

'A doctor! This man needs a doctor!' she called to the people gathering round. There was an excited babble of voices in response and soon an older man came purposefully to her side, and by his professional manner she knew him to be medically trained.

When a uniformed official joined him, mobile phone in hand, she leaned over to ask, 'Can I help?' But the man she assumed to be a doctor merely shook his head and smiled as he returned his stethoscope to his pocket.

'Thank you, no, ambulance comes,' he said, his attention on his patient whose eyes were just beginning to flicker.

*   *   *

The oval face of the fair-haired girl seemed to draw nearer as Rafel's vision slowly cleared, and through the haze her features took shape for a moment before she disappeared from view. He attempted to lift his head, follow her, but strength failed him as a thousand hammers pounded his brain. The circle of faces above closed in, he tried to speak but his tongue was leaden and his lips refused to form the words.

He managed to utter a faint, 'Where am I?' and heard a comforting response in his own language, Catalan.

'Do not alarm yourself, Señor, you have merely fainted. Most probably the sudden

6

change of climate.'

A uniformed officer gave a nod of agreement. 'Now we have his identity, can I leave this with you, doctor? I would appreciate a full report from the hospital,' he added before moving off to keep the curious onlookers at bay, leaving the doctor to continue with a further examination.

Still Rafel couldn't respond or object with any clarity when it was decided he be taken for more detailed observation.

'I need to admit you to hospital for tests, purely routine,' the doctor said with a quick smile. 'You haven't a history of heart trouble?'

Rafel shook his head and grimaced.

'Not to my knowledge,' came his weak reply. 'If you will just allow me to rest—no need for the hospital. And my luggage, there are two . . .'

'Don't worry, Professor, the matter has been attended to,' the doctor assured him, catching the attention of a young airport attendant who came forward to place a suitcase beside the bench.

'The other one, a packing case!' Rafel said feebly.

The doctor frowned.

'A packing case, did you say?'

He managed to nod, increasing the hammering in his head.

'Si, si, I must have it!'

'Keep calm, Professor. I will send the boy to

look for it.'

A feeling of unease crept into Rafel's troubled mind, and when the youth returned empty-handed, even after a senior official had been sought, his anxiety was intensified.

'There was no baggage left on the conveyor after your flight had been cleared,' the man declared with certainty.

'I know it left London, I saw it being loaded,' Rafel insisted, raising himself on to one elbow.

But the official merely shook his head.

'We have searched everywhere, Señor. It is not possible such an object could escape our notice. Perhaps your illness has affected your memory. You may have a previous journey in mind or . . .'

With renewed energy Rafel exploded. 'Of course not, man! It is a wooden packing case—I must have it!'

'I repeat, it is impossible to find your luggage if it is nor here, Señor, so I will give you a form to complete. I trust you will make a good recovery.'

Dismayed, Rafel watched the man walk quickly away.

'I did have another piece of luggage,' he groaned to the doctor. 'Surely you believe me.'

'Si, si, but perhaps someone has taken it by mistake,' the doctor consoled.

'Impossible! Please allow me to look for myself.'

'It will be returned to you in due course. Meanwhile, I suggest you remain still until the ambulance arrives,' the doctor advised.

To Rafel's dismay, he found his legs wouldn't support him when he swung his feet to the ground. He was forced to succumb as waves of nausea rose again.

The guitar had been stolen he realised dismally as he lay back, closing his eyes against the bright lights of the airport hall. Someone had taken the precious instrument when he'd collapsed, yet who knew what the packing case contained?

Suddenly, he opened his eyes and gasped, 'Yes, the blonde girl! I must see her!'

'Do not worry, Professor, you can contact her later,' the doctor soothed. 'We'll soon have you well again.'

Rafel gripped the man's sleeve.

'But you don't understand. She was on the plane!'

The doctor's expression of tolerance was replaced by one of relief when the ambulance came to a screeching halt outside.

'Si, si, all in good time, Professor,' he murmured thankfully.

Rafel struggled to convince the medical team he was well enough to go home by taxi, but his efforts were rewarded by a return to semi-consciousness before they drove into the busy city in the direction of the hospital.

Once she had her suitcase safely on a trolley, Fiona glanced back along the airport hall, giving a sigh of relief when she saw the ambulance crew arrive. She had been concerned over the ailing man but hoped whoever had been sent to meet her had not tired of waiting to transport her to the villa of her late uncle which she had recently inherited.

She had last seen the villa as a child, travelling here with her mother, almost twenty years ago. The memory had blurred, though this unexpected inheritance following uncle Jaume's accidental death had increased her curiosity about what her mother had once described as the foreign side of the family.

Pity about the guitar, she thought. Even though Jaume Vancells was no longer alive, it would have been satisfying to have brought his grandfather's instrument back to its original home. Sadly, she couldn't possibly have paid the price it reached at the sale. Such a coincidence, the purchaser had travelled on the same plane and then been taken ill. She wondered if the guitar had travelled with him.

'We would like to take a sample of your blood, Professor, then perhaps we can solve this mystery illness of yours.'

Rafel flinched as a needle slid into his vein, the sharp pain jogging his memory.

'Not again,' he complained dazedly.

The physician paused, peering over his spectacles.

'Again? They took a blood sample at the airport?'

'I think so,' Rafel said, attempting to rouse himself.

'Are you sure? The doctor didn't mention anything.'

'No? Strange, but I have a feeling it was before I fainted.'

The doctor's brows rose.

'Interesting. Tell me more.'

Rafel frowned.

'I seem to recall it happening soon after I left the plane. Something stabbed my thigh. No, perhaps I'm imagining things.'

The other man emptied his syringe and sealed the sample bottle with practised efficiency before handing it to his assistant, urging him to make haste to the laboratory. Then, returning his attention to the bed, he pulled back the sheets to scan his patient's lower limbs.

'Ah, yes!' he exclaimed once he'd eased Rafel onto his side. 'I see a puncture to the skin here and it's the mark of a hypodermic. You have not imagined it, Señor!'

'Thank goodness! I was beginning to think I

11

was hallucinating. But who could have done that? Why me?'

'You tell me, Professor. The reason for your collapse was a mystery. However, I am sure the blood test will tell us something positive. I'm curious to know what was used.'

'So am I, and why. I'm beginning to believe it is connected with the disappearance of my packing case,' he declared, then fell silent, concentrating his thoughts on each moment after he left the plane.

'I want to give you a sedative, but if there is anything more you can tell me it might help,' the doctor urged.

'Yes, there was a blonde girl. She was at the auction sale, but she went ahead so someone else must be involved, maybe an accomplice.'

'Don't worry,' the doctor advised. 'It will all come back to you in time.'

'But the guitar was valuable and she seemed desperate to possess it. Yes, I'm convinced it has been stolen.'

'Well, if you are right, it is a case for the police.'

*　　　*　　　*

During the early hours of the following morning, Rafel awoke and stretched full length along the bed, feeling his strength return. His thoughts immediately went over the events that had led up to his present predicament. Hearing a slight movement nearby, he turned to see a heavily clad figure rise from a chair in the corner of the room. The sister bowed her head and left, soon to return accompanied by the doctor who had administered the sedative earlier.

'Bon dia, Professor,' he greeted in Catalan, coming briskly to the bedside to extend a steadying hand as Rafel pulled himself up to a sitting position. 'You shouldn't feel too bad this morning. I gave you something to counteract the after-effects of the drug someone pumped into you.'

He smiled and went on to reel off the name of the drug that had been so deftly introduced into Rafel's thigh at the airport.

'It is very effective, and now we must endeavour to discover the reason it was administered,' the doctor continued. And with an apologetic shrug, he added, 'The police had to be informed, of course, and they will be calling on you, but I deferred their visit until you had recovered from this unfortunate incident.'

Rafel's mind reeled as his suspicions increased. The fact that someone had gone to such lengths to part him from his luggage was alarming. Deep in thought he sank back on the pillows as the doctor took his wrist.

'Your pulse is steady,' he reported. 'Don't worry, we'll soon have you fit again. By the way, I took the liberty of informing your

13

family. Didn't divulge the real reason for your delay, of course. Told thcm heat exhaustion.'

'My mother, she would have hysterics!'

The doctor smiled and slipped a stethoscope to his ears.

'I suggest you remain here until midday when I will arrange for someone to drive you home. Sister has brushed you clothes so you should arrive reasonably presentable. You appeared to have been in a drunken brawl when they brought your here last night.'

A sparkle lit up Rafel's dark eyes.

'That accounts for my king-sized hangover this morning!' he laughed. 'But would you credit one gin and tonic with having such a drastic effect!'

'Well, take it easy for the next forty-eight hours. The police will take care of the rest. I see you have a nasty bruise on the site of the needle puncture which means whoever administered that syringe was in a hurry to drive it home!'

Sliding down between the crisp white sheets Rafel's thoughts returned to the previous evening. He was convinced the blonde girl had been involved. She was the only one to know of his purchase and she had wanted the guitar for herself. Her look of sheer disappointment when she had dropped out of the bidding told him that much. But would she have taken the risk to seize his luggage whilst he lay unconscious?

He recalled seeing his name on the list she carried yet found it hard to perceive such an innocent-looking girl could be so devious. He remonstrated with himself for not furthering his attempt to view her passport more closely. It was imperative he find her, and soon.

Filled with frustration he fell into a restless doze, and almost two hours passed before he was fully awakened by a smiling sister in flowing white robes, making little sound as she crossed the highly-polished floor.

'Good day, Señor Professor. I am afraid the police are already here. Inspector Ferrer wishes to speak with you.'

'Thank you, I feel well enough to receive him now.'

Within moments, a tall and solidly built man came into the room, followed by another, much younger, who hesitated by the doorway. Unbidden, the first seated himself by the bed, grunting as he settled his large frame on to the small, wooden chair. He nodded a silent greeting, and taking a notebook from his pocket immediately plunged into a tirade of questions based on the few facts he had already gleaned from the doctor.

'You returned from London yesterday, I understand.'

'That is correct, Inspector.'

'And you state that a hypodermic needle entered your left thigh at Barcelona airport. Is this so, Professor?'

15

'Si, it is.'

'Can you recall the persons immediately behind you at the time of the assault?' the inspector went on briskly.

Rafel shook his head and went on to relate, once more, all he could recall of the previous evening. But it was when the inspector reached the point in his questioning of who else amongst the disembarking passengers could have knowledge of what the packing case contained that he hesitated, suddenly and unaccountably reluctant to involve the girl.

As he had dozed her face had returned to his memory, time and time again. Her tearful expression in the saleroom haunted him, yet he couldn't bring himself to mention her connection with the incident. The feeling she couldn't possibly have knowingly been partner to anything unscrupulous grew stronger, and again he shook his head. He would attempt to trace the girl himself, and if she could offer a plausible explanation then there was no point in involving her with the police.

'You have given us very little to work on, Professor,' the inspector complained. 'However, I can assure you we shall do our best. You will be at home for the next few days?'

'Of course, and I hope you succeed in tracing my beautiful instrument, also to discover who drugged me.'

'And why? For a guitar?' the inspector said,

sounding puzzled.

'It is valued at more than four million pesetas!' Rafel exclaimed.

'I assume it is insured?'

'Si, but it is of great sentimental value to me.'

Ferrer's eyes rolled to the ceiling as he rose from the creaking chair when his aide sprang forward to open the door.

Distressed as he was over the loss of his precious instrument, as the door closed behind the two men, Rafel breathed a sigh of relief and swung his legs over the edge of the bed. The thought of that dark red passport bearing the name Fiona Max . . . spurred him into action.

*   *   *

At midday, in an old villa near Castelldefels, Fiona Maxwell took off her wide-brimmed hat, placing it on the hall table.

'Do go through, Mr Grey,' she said to the middle-aged man who had transported her from the airport the evening before. 'I'll bring in a cool drink.'

'I would appreciate that, Miss Maxwell,' he said as he surveyed the fine furniture in the spacious hall. 'Hope you haven't found our tour too tiring. It was too late when we arrived here last evening, but I was sure you would want to see what lies beyond the boundary of

17

the property you have inherited. The fences are in rather a mess as you would notice, and expensive to replace, but you can rest assured I will assist with the legalities once you decide what you intend to do with the place. Your uncle always valued my advice.'

'Yes, I'm going to need someone to advise me, but I'm surprised my uncle never mentioned you, particularly as you and he were friends. Though I must admit, he wrote to my mother only occasionally.'

Fiona smiled as she entered the kitchen. A cooling glass of sangria topped with a slice of freshly cut lemon should quench her thirst, yet she felt it was poor compensation for the time and trouble Herbert Grey, the property advisor, had taken. Suddenly, she heard the shrill note of a woman's voice coming from the hall.

'I am arriving early, Señor,' she heard, 'but the Señorita Maxwell was not in the house.'

Fiona rushed from the kitchen to find a dark-haired woman standing by the salon door.

'I am Fiona Maxwell. What is it?'

'This woman claims she was Señor Vancells' housekeeper,' Mr Grey explained.

'Si, I am Rosa,' she said, turning her ashen face in Fiona's direction to reveal blood oozing from a wound to her head.

'Oh dear, you are hurt!' Fiona gasped. 'What happened?'

'This morning I come to meet you, Señorita,' Rosa said in halting English. 'Somebody breaks in the house, but you are not here so I call the police.'

Seeing the newcomer was quite shocked, Fiona led her over to a chair.

'Yes, I have been out, taking a look around this place,' she said. 'You see, I only arrived yesterday evening.'

'Probably just some hooligan,' Grey suggested. 'No need to involve the police. Better you cancel the call.'

'But we can't be sure,' Fiona broke in sharply. 'Perhaps you will be kind enough to bring Rosa a glass of water whilst I attend to that wound.'

'These people love a drama, believe me,' he mumbled as he went in the direction of the kitchen.

Surprised by his lack of sympathy, Fiona went upstairs to find clean dressings for Rosa's wound, but in the doorway of her room she came to an abrupt halt. The wardrobe door stood open and she saw her once neatly hung dresses were strewn across the floor. Clothing cascaded from each drawer of the chest standing by the opposite wall, and even the bedclothes had been dragged back. Someone had made a very thorough search.

A shudder ran through her as she found a clean bandage and cotton wool. Mr Grey may not realise it but Rosa had acted wisely. This was not merely a case of Latin hysterics.

'My room has been ransacked,' she announced on her return. 'Thank goodness the police have been notified.'

'That is unfortunate,' Grey remarked. 'Are you sure?'

'Of course I'm sure!' she cried. 'And I hope Rosa can describe the intruder to the police when they get here.'

'I'll take her to a hospital,' he offered with unexpected concern.

'No need, it is fairly superficial. There is a nasty bump appearing, but don't worry, I am a nurse.'

'Then perhaps you will deal with it,' he suggested. 'I have rather pressing business to attend to. I'll ring you.'

'But the police may not speak English,' Fiona began to protest, but Grey had already left, and soon afterwards came the sound of footsteps followed by a tap on the salon door.

'Good day, Señorita,' said the solidly built man standing in the doorway. 'Inspector Ferrer,' he announced, coming to peer at the dressing on Rosa's head. 'Señora, you mentioned nothing of this when you telephoned.'

Once he had ascertained the identity of those present he commenced his questioning of Rosa as he looked down on her shaking form. He listened and nodded, then motioned his assistant to take notes before summoning

20

the forensic department on his mobile telephone. Addressing Fiona, he asked in his heavily accented English, 'Do you see anything is missing?'

'I don't think so, Inspector,' she replied, 'though I'm not yet familiar with the place. I arrived only yesterday.'

Ferrer then turned his attention to Rosa.

Perhaps you can describe your assailant for me while we wait for the doctor.'

At the mention of her attacker, Rosa began to tremble afresh.

'I was in the vestibule, I did not see his face,' she sobbed. 'He came behind me, put his hand over my mouth.'

'Think again, Señora,' Ferrer urged. 'Surely you noticed something about the man. Was he tall, dark, young or old?'

'I believe he was not tall, Inspector, but he was dark. I saw the hair on the back of his hand. It was very black!'

'Si, si, go on, what did you do?'

'I only saw his hands,' she wailed, 'not his face.'

'There must be something else, Señora, think!'

Rose took a shuddering breath.

'Ah, yes, part of his finger is missing. His index finger—left hand—I remember now!'

'Good!' he encouraged. 'And what did he say to you?'

'He asked me where something is. I don't

know what he is meaning, but then I managed to pull his hand away and I scream.'

'Si, si, and then?'

'He hit me with something hard. I was very dizzy. I thought he is in the house so I am running to a pubic telephone to call for help. Did I do right?'

'Of course, you have been very brave,' he agreed, pausing as a vehicle drew up outside. 'Ah, here are my men. They will examine downstairs first which will allow you to use the kitchen. I am sure you are in need of a coffee, or perhaps something a little stronger,' he suggested, eyeing the tray and glasses, then queried, 'You do not intend to leave the house for the next few days?'

'No, Inspector, but it has been quite a shock. I'm inclined to feel a little nervous in these unfamiliar surroundings,' Fiona pointed out. 'Can I be sure it won't happen again?'

Ferrer's bushy brows rose. 'Let me assure you, Señorita, one of my men will be keeping an eye on this villa.'

'And I shall make sure the doors are locked,' she said, relaxing until she remembered the invitation she had received before she left London. 'Oh, just a moment, Inspector, I almost forgot. I'm to attend a concert in Barcelona tomorrow evening, in honour of my late uncle's work. His compositions are to be played by a local guitarist, I couldn't possibly miss it.'

He gave a brief smile. 'No, of course, it is the Vancells concert. I'll arrange for a car to take you. When do you wish to leave?'

'I must reach the theatre by nine-thirty, no later.'

CHAPTER 2

It was late afternoon when a servant of the Pujol household helped Rafel alight from his taxi. His mother, Elenor, waited impatiently on the threshold of their home, a large house near the centre of the city, standing beside one of Barcelona's wide, tree-lined streets.

'Rafel! You look so ill!' she cried in shocked tones. 'I warned you London is a tiring place. The doctor said . . .'

'Mama, it was nothing, merely the sudden change in climate. London was cool and I had a great deal of business to attend to,' he said, stooping to brush his lips on each of her cheeks in turn.

'Come in,' she said, 'and tell me exactly what happened.'

'Everyone is making too much fuss,' he replied guardedly. 'As the doctor told you, I merely fainted. Now I must make up for lost time and write notes from my London visit.'

'The doctor rang me personally, he was most concerned. He recommends you rest and I insist you take his advice.'

'Mama, I am over thirty years old, not a child any more.'

She threw up her hands in despair then, leaning towards him, said softly, 'Now, tell me about London, and the blonde girl.'

'The blonde girl,' he echoed, meeting his mother's dark-eyed scrutiny with difficulty. 'What a strange request.'

'You may look at me with those innocent eyes of yours, but you didn't have to go away on the pretext of business!'

'I did go on business, you know that.'

She gave him a knowing smile.

'Actually, it was the doctor who mentioned her when I received the first message from the airport. He assumed you were together.'

'I assure you, she was only a fellow passenger.'

'But she was sufficiently concerned to remain beside you until you regained consciousness. Naturally, he thought she had travelled with you, especially as you asked for her before they took you to the hospital.'

Confused but unable to divulge the whole story, Rafel shook his head.

'Perhaps I was a trifle delirious,' he offered finally, then fell silent, pondering over the reason the girl had stayed whilst he remained unconscious.

Maybe she had been anxious to learn what he revealed to the doctor, or the police, worried that he might incriminate her. Perhaps there was more to Miss Max . . . than he had allowed himself to believe. He must not forget—she had his name listed, a fact which had almost slipped his mind as he lay in hospital. But now he recalled that stupid little case and it all came back. He had to trace her.

In the quiet atmosphere of his study, Rafel thought about the girl. She had looked so innocent he couldn't believe her to be involved in anything underhand. Or was he allowing himself to be deceived by a pretty face? But why had she waited until he regained consciousness? Dare he hope it was out of genuine concern?

He considered the motive for her journey. Was she on holiday, or on business? To him, the latter seemed more likely as it was improbable anyone going off to soak up the sun for a week or so would attend a sale of valuable musical instruments which it had appeared she could ill afford, leaving herself little time to reach the airport.

Deciding to enquire if her name was listed on a return flight, he telephoned the airport, but no-one would divulge the names on any passenger list. He reconsidered discussing her with the police. Perhaps they could supply an answer to the question that troubled him now.

Early the following morning, he made the call but Inspector Ferrer was already out on a case, and it was with a curious feeling of relief that he replaced the receiver. He had battled with his conscience during a restless night. Just thinking about the blonde girl disturbed him, but was he being sensible, concealing the facts from the inspector?

'You are very pale,' his mother remarked

when he joined her for breakfast, and throughout the meal she continued anxiously, 'What is this illness you picked up in England?'

'It is nothing serious,' he insisted, pushing back his chair. 'Now I must go to the department. I won't be away too long.'

Glancing at his watch as he left, he made for the main thoroughfare. For some unaccountable reason he was glad Ferrer had not been available and decided to take a walk via the cathedral to watch the traditional dancing of the Sardana, an occasion which drew him there most Sundays. But this morning he would take it easy, not partake in the dancing until the doctor's prescribed forty-eight hours had passed.

The traffic was light and the streets had been freshly sprayed with water, settling the dust and releasing a faint perfume from the trees bordering the roadway. He felt a little tired but noticed none of the dreadful after-effects of the drug as he strode towards the Gothic Quarter. His spirits lifted, he took off his jacket, hooking it over his shoulder on one finger, and slackened his pace to glance in the shop windows as he strolled along.

In this area the shops stocked merchandise of high quality. He paused to admire a light linen suit, speculating on the cost as he moved on to the next window. Perhaps he would buy a slim wallet for the doctor who had attended him so efficiently. He spotted a few possibilities then, as his eyes travelled over the display, they widened suddenly and he pressed closer to the glass. There, on the centre shelf, lay an object he recognised instantly, a case in shining leather with an unusual gilt handle, a case which appeared to be identical to the one carried by the girl on the plane!

He bent forward to read the printed card beside it. *'Exclusive'* it said. *'Items on display designed and made on the premises.'*

Stroking his chin between forefinger and thumb, he straightened. Had her case been made here? His intention to watch the dancing in the cathedral square forgotten, he decided to go inside and make enquiries.

A smiling young female assistant greeted him as he entered.

'May I help you?'

'Si, I am interested in the case on display in your window, the one with an unusual handle on the centre shelf.'

'Ah, si, Señor, you have excellent taste. This is one of our exclusive designs . . .'

'Not quite exclusive,' he broke in. 'I have seen another, only recently.'

She flushed and smiled.

'Ah, and the lady who carried it would be the mother of our most respected mayor. We made only three, you see, for exclusive clientele.'

He raised one dark brow.

'And the other customer, could she be English?'

The assistant hesitated as a more senior lady came swiftly to her side to announce coolly, 'I will attend to the gentleman, Celia,' and addressing Rafel, the elegant newcomer enquired, 'Shall I get it from the window, Señor?'

'Before you do, can you tell me if this particular model is made for export?'

'No, Señor, our business is not export or mass production.'

'Then I would like to know who purchased the other one. I'm sure you will record the names of your clientele in such an exclusive boutique.'

'Certainly, but I would never divulge this information.'

'Not even if I were to purchase this one?' he cajoled, smiling widely.

'Not even if you were to purchase the whole stock!' she shot back.

'Please, it is essential I contact the lady,' he appealed. 'It is urgent.'

He head wobbled slightly when she replied with a hint of triumph, 'Actually, the customer was a man,' and with a curl of her red lips, continued, 'and if it is imperative you find this woman, I suggest you look elsewhere!'

Deflated, he left the shop and proceeded towards the school of music to prepare for his forthcoming lecture but soon found he was unable to concentrate and pushed his papers aside. He had to increase his efforts to trace this girl. Could she be a tourist? Should he visit the popular attractions? Was there a chance she may be there?

At noon, he found a quiet bar and ordered an aperitif. Up to now his wanderings had been futile. He had scanned every passing group of tourists and spent an hour in the cathedral with his eyes fixed on the huge doorway. Now, weary and crestfallen, he contemplated an early lunch and reached for the menu. Having made his choice, he was looking around for the waitress when he spotted a young lady entering whom he recognised as the assistant in the shop he had visited earlier. Smiling, he rose to his feet.

'May I offer you a drink?'

She hesitated a moment before accepting.

'Graçias, Señor. Coffee please.'

Indicating she join him, he enquired, 'Are you dining here?'

'Oh no, Señor, it is much too expensive.'

'Then be my guest, please. I caused you such embarrassment this morning, I feel I owe you this much.'

'Ah, it is always like that. She's so bossy.'

'I realise you would have been more charming and helpful, Celia.' He smiled. 'She had no business to interfere.'

'You know my name!'

There was a twinkle in his dark eyes as he

replied, 'I heard it in the shop. How could I forget?'

The girl's cheeks went pink and she lowered her eyes.

'I would have helped you, Señor, if she hadn't been there.'

'Then whilst you study the menu, I shall order wine. Then perhaps we can have a quiet talk, eh, Celia?'

'But I don't really know you, Señor, and I wouldn't want my employer to learn of it. She may not approve.'

'You are not expected back until four-thirty, surely? And as we are already acquainted, why don't we enjoy each other's company? It is not every day I have the pleasure of dining with such an attractive young lady,' he added persuasively.

Wordlessly, she gazed at him as he gave the waiter their order.

'To your health, Celia,' he said, raising his glass. 'Now, what was it you were going to tell me?'

'Ah, si, that special case,' she replied, lowering her voice. 'It was purchased by Jaume Vancells as a gift for his niece.'

His eyes narrowed. 'Vancells?'

'Si, you know, Vancells, the musician.'

'But he died almost a month ago!'

'Si, I know. In fact, there's a memorial concert of his music in Barcelona tonight. We have a poster in the shop.'

'I didn't notice,' he groaned. 'Do you know where?'

'In a private house, near the Theatre Liceu, I think, but only by invitation. I can't remember any more.'

'Celia, you're an angel!' he exclaimed, leaning over to plant a kiss on her forehead. 'Now, enjoy your meal. I have an urgent appointment so I must leave you quite soon.'

She stared at him in surprise.

'Shall I see you again?'

'Celia, whenever we chance to meet in the same restaurant, you dine with me!'

His mother greeted him on his return, her tone of disapproval bringing a glint of amusement to his eyes.

'The police telephoned when you were out!'

'Mother, I am not a criminal! What do they want?'

'Did you not telephone them earlier?'

'Si, only to ask if they had recovered my luggage,' he lied convincingly. 'There was a mix-up at the airport.'

For the second time, Rafel telephoned Ferrer's office to enquire about his luggage. He sighed. Little progress had been made, but could he secure an invitation for tonight's recital?

*   *   *

In the villa at Castelldefels, Fiona Maxwell's

expression was one of disappointment as she spoke into the telephone.

'But, Mr Grey, I thought it was all arranged,' she protested. 'I need to discuss this property if I'm to stay.'

'I realise that,' came his brisk reply, 'but I must fly back tomorrow. Sudden business appointment, you understand.'

'When do you expect to return?'

'Difficult to say, but that is business for you,' Grey replied. 'Actually, I rang to ask if the police had been.'

'Yes, and there is an officer watching the place. But what concerns me most is this property, and what I must do about my employment. You see, I'm bound to give at least one month's notice . . . Mr Grey?'

She realised he had hung up and replaced her own receiver none too gently. Going into the bedroom where Rosa was resting, she related her conversation with Herbert Grey.

'This man I do not like,' Rosa stated emphatically.

Fiona smiled.

'But why? He's been very helpful but I expect he is busy, and he did meet me at the airport to bring me here.'

'Pah! My brother would have done it—anything for Señor Jaume. He loved his music—you have heard it?'

'I'm afraid not. I was only five when my mother brought me here, too young to appreciate my uncle's talent. My memories of him are not very clear, and I've never heard his music played so I am really looking forward to this evening. Did Mr Grey come to hear him play? I believe they were friends.'

Rosa's expression changed. 'I can not believe Señor Vancells gave him permission to come here.'

'But he told me he was a close friend of my uncle and the London solicitor had asked him to show me round the place.'

Rosa shook her head.

'This I do not believe. I never see him before your uncle dies. Today is the first time.'

*   *   *

Taking a glass of sparkling wine from the tray as he entered the crowded hall, Rafel paused, his gaze travelling over the heads of the assembled guests. Because of that strange little case and the fact that Vancells had purchased one of only three made, Rafel considered there was a chance the girl on the plane could be the niece of whom Celia had spoken. Hopeful of making contact with her he had contrived an invitation, and now, engrossed in the purpose of his visit, he listened to the mixed comments of music lovers standing nearby.

'Unusual arrangement. Progressive and exciting,' he heard.

'Jaume Vancells still lives through his music,' another declared. 'Devoted himself to it after he lost his father.'

Suddenly aware the man beside him was speaking, he collected his thoughts.

'You are most welcome to look round,' the man invited. 'We have many beautiful paintings here.'

'Gracias,' said Rafel, following the man's gesturing hand indicating the crowded adjoining room.

He edged forward to get a better view when, quite unexpectedly, his glance fell on an object, which lay on a small table just inside the room, a strange little casc with a gilt handle!

'Gracias,' he repeated softly as he caught sight of the girl standing beneath a large painting, her back turned in his direction, the light gleaming on her smooth fair hair. For a moment he couldn't believe his luck. He hadn't expected it to be easy, but now he had found her how was he to tackle the situation? He saw her reach for the case as if about to move away and knew this was an opportunity he couldn't afford to miss. With a look of determination on his solemn face, he advanced quickly towards her.

'Good evening, Señorita,' he said and she turned, her eyes meeting his for a second until recognition dawned.

She smiled.

'Oh, I remember. You were taken ill at the airport. What a coincidence, meeting you here this evening!'

'A coincidence indeed, but this time I intend to remain conscious!' he countered with a short laugh.

She frowned and shot him a curious look.

'I've just realised, you spoke to me in English. How did you know?'

'I heard you speak to the steward on the plane, and I noticed your passport, Miss . . . er?'

'Maxwell,' she supplied hesitantly. 'Fiona Maxwell.'

'So, tell me, Miss Maxwell, which treasure have you got designs on this evening?' he enquired in a voice edged with sarcasm, and saw her frown slightly before a quick smile returned to her lovely face.

'This place is full of treasures,' she enthused, indicating a gilt-framed landscape on another wall, 'but that is my favourite.'

Rafel didn't follow her pointing finger but allowed his eyes to linger on the perfect profile of her unturned face and the smoothness of her cheek with its delicate hint of rose, then down to the scooped neckline of the simple black dress she wore. He had to steel himself against a surge of unexpected emotion and tore his gaze away knowing he must not allow her beauty to influence him. Even so, how could he accuse her here, amongst all these people?

'Miss Maxwell,' he began, 'may I enquire what brought you to Catalonia?'

She looked up, silencing him with a quick lift of her fine brows.

'First, I think I should know your name, and why you are here this evening?'

'My name!' he rejoined with an incredulous laugh. 'You ask my name!'

Her eyes darkened. 'I don't like your manner, Señor!'

'I don't believe this!' he cried. 'Surely, you can't deny that you have my name on a list in your case.'

'Don't be ridiculous!' she hissed and drew away.

'Not so fast,' he said. 'I think we should stop this charade and you speak the truth!'

'Look, I don't know who you are, but . . .'

'Then perhaps you can explain,' he pursued harshly, 'why you keep a record of my name?'

'You're quite mad!' she cried, her eyes flashing. 'If you don't go away I shall call the director!'

'Please do, and perhaps he can enlighten me about your suspicious behaviour.'

'How dare you, Señor! I have no idea to what you are referring.'

'I think you have, and perhaps I should warn you the police have become involved,' he said with cool authority.

'The police?'

'Si, they are as curious as I why my luggage was whisked away as I lay unconscious. You can't deny it, you were there at the time.'

She stared at him in alarm.

'I saw you were ill, but I know nothing of your luggage, believe me.'

He noticed the indignation had gone from her expression and she now appeared filled with concern. Was she merely an innocent traveller? But his name, he had seen it for himself.

'Perhaps the name Rafel Pujol means something to you,' he prompted.

'Rafel Pujol, the professor? You are . . .'

'You seem surprised.'

'Yes, I am, but why are you questioning me? You outbid me in London so I would have thought you well satisfied.'

'That, Señorita, is not the point. The question is, where is the guitar now? And if you have been inveigled into doing something illegal, it would be wiser for you to admit it.'

'You mean you haven't got it?' she asked with a blank stare. 'Why not? What happened?'

He decided if she could give an acceptable reason for having his name listed, he had no alternative but to trust her. So, refilling their glasses, he led her to a seat by the entrance.

'It was a list of names sent to me by my uncle, just before he was killed,' she explained. 'They were all students of his father, people whom he thought may be able to assist in tracing the instrument which was stolen from him some years ago.'

'And his name?'

'Vancells, Jaume Vancells.'

'So it is of sentimental value to you, the reason you wanted it so much.'

He gave a thoughtful smile.

'I remember Vancells—a great musician, classical, too.'

Her eyes widened.

'You knew him? Oh, that's wonderful!'

'His father gave me lessons, years ago,' Rafel told her and nodded towards the salon. 'His son had an entirely different style, although, hearing his compositions this evening, I realise he had quite a talent of his own.'

She sighed and looked around.

'I assume you are here because of your interest in music?'

Rafel smiled. 'Have you not yet learned of the Catalan's great love of the arts? But in addition to my love of music, my real reason for being here tonight was to find you.'

'I see, but now I've explained why I had your name listed, perhaps you will believe I had no ulterior motive. And now it is your turn to tell me how you lost the guitar.'

'Lost the guitar!' he echoed incredulously. 'I didn't lose it. It was stolen at the airport. A very ordinary packing case of which you assure me you know absolutely nothing.'

Sensing a hint of disbelief in his tone, she looked up to retort, 'Señor Pujol, in addition to the Catalan's great love of the arts you have also inherited his typical passion for argument! What must I do to convince you of my innocence?'

'Forgive me, but I am extremely annoyed by the loss. I would give anything to have it back in my possession.'

'So would I, though I couldn't have paid your price. My uncle had great difficulty in tracing it until he received a journal from England and found it was listed amongst other instruments due to be auctioned. The maker's name was almost unknown in that year, so he was sure it must be the one.'

'It was made by a local craftsman, Sesrovires, I believe.'

'Yes, that's right.'

She smiled, but when her attention was caught by the director, she murmured, 'Do excuse me a moment.'

'May I speak with you later? There are a few small details you may be able to help me with. Perhaps over dinner?' he added hopefully as a hand touched his sleeve. He turned to find a colleague standing there.

He started to make the introductions but found she had already disappeared into the main salon.

'Ah, now you must wait for the finale. You have excellent taste, by friend. I caught a

40

glimpse of her as I came in. English?' his colleague asked.

Rafel nodded and they returned to their seats, lending a professional ear to the performance for later discussion.

After the final piece was played, Rafel searched for Fiona Maxwell's fair head over the crowd but she was nowhere to be seen. With rising anxiety he skirted the room, coming to a halt by the director's chair.

'If you are looking for the Señorita,' the director said, 'I'm afraid she has already left. Understandable, of course, particularly in view of the recent trouble at the villa.'

Rafel frowned and turned away to hide his disappointment. What was this trouble the director spoke of, and why hadn't she mentioned it? Or was it merely a ruse on her part to avoid any further questions? He wondered if the frustration he felt was entirely connected with his inability to question her. She was an extremely attractive young woman.

'You look disappointed,' his colleague commented as they left. 'Have you not made an arrangement to meet her again?'

'I didn't have the opportunity,' Rafel replied, then added with certainty, 'but I can soon remedy that!'

CHAPTER 3

'You must continue to visit your sister, Rosa,' Fiona insisted, 'otherwise she will worry.'

'I should not leave you after what is happening here,' the housekeeper protested.

'Yesterday, Inspector Ferrer promised me he will have this house under surveillance.'

'Ah, but have you seen anyone?'

'No, but I expect he is in one of the stationary cars along the road. Don't worry, Rosa, I'll be quite safe.'

Shortly after Rosa departed, Fiona heard a car pull up outside and crossed to the window in time to see a tall figure wearing a light suit striding along the path. Drawing back the heavy bolt, she opened the door as Rafel was about to knock.

Inclining his dark head slightly he said, 'I assume this is not inconvenient, Señorita? You left early last night before I could speak with you regarding my dilemma at the airport.'

'Sorry, I had to go, my transport was waiting. Even so, I doubt I can be of further assistance, Señor. I already have told you everything I know.'

'Please, there could be something, however insignificant it may have seemed at the time.'

Seeing how desperate he was, she felt obliged to invite him inside.

42

'Perhaps we should discuss the matter indoors.'

'I am grateful for your time, particularly after your recent trouble here.'

About to lead him into the salon, she hesitated, her expression wary.

'How do you know that?'

'The director mentioned it last night. Don't worry, I'm not aware of the details, unless you wish to enlighten me.'

Her apprehension subsided.

'We had a break-in. The housekeeper was injured and my room ransacked,' she told him bluntly, indicating he should take a seat. 'So you see, you are not the only one with a mystery to solve.'

'Indeed, I am not! When was this?'

'Rosa discovered it yesterday morning, whilst I was out.'

'And whilst I lay in a hospital bed!' he exclaimed with a short laugh.

'Sorry, I had intended to ask. Was it anything serious?'

He compressed his lips thoughtfully.

'Well, serious enough, and I suspect whoever inflicted it made off with my luggage. A drug was administered by hypodermic.'

She looked at him, aghast.

'I see. I can appreciate why you're here, but exactly what is it you wish to know?'

'What happened after I became unconscious?' he asked. 'Did you see anyone take my packing case from the conveyor?'

'No, my attention was centred on you and I immediately called for assistance. You were slumped at my feet, out cold, so I wasn't aware of anything else at the time.'

Noting his disappointment she rose to pour two glassfuls of wine as she continued.

'In fact, I didn't collect my own luggage until you were in the hands of the airport medical attendant. By that time mine was the only case left on the carousel.'

'Forgive me, I must appear ungrateful. It was kind of you to seek help. You understand, I remember seeing your face as I regained consciousness, but then you disappeared, hence my suspicions. Tell me, why did you stay until I recovered?'

'I trained as a nurse so, naturally, I was concerned.'

'Good heavens!' he exclaimed softly. 'And to think I almost reported you to Inspector Ferrer.'

She shot him a quick glance. 'Inspector Ferrer? What a coincidence. He's the man who is handling things here.'

His eyes widened. 'Ah, so you have met the inspector. He is a shrewd fellow with a reputation for getting his man.'

She twirled the stem of her glass, her expression reflective as she murmured, 'Let us hope so.'

Rafel raised his glass.

44

'To the inspector!' he said, sampling its contents before he continued, 'Incidentally, you haven't yet told me what brought you to Catalonia?'

She shrugged. 'It was because I had inherited this place. I'd had a letter from a solicitor in Barcelona informing me of my uncle's death. Unfortunately, I'd moved house before it arrived so didn't receive the news in time to attend the funeral. I felt really sad about that as I believe I was his closest living relative, though it is years since I came here with my mother, who also was Catalan.'

'Your uncle's death was a great loss to the musical world,' he remarked. 'A most unfortunate accident.'

'I expect you would know him better than I did. You see, I was only a child when we last met.' Her expression grew sad as she added, 'Now I have lost the only relative I had.'

'You are not married? No boyfriend in England?'

'No-one special. A few friends, of course.'

'Ah well, you are very young . . .'

'I'm twenty-three,' she broke in indignantly, then laughed. 'For more than a year now I've led an independent life.'

'I see. So you intend to live here, in this house?'

She wrinkled her nose. 'I quite like it, but I understand from the agent who met me at the airport there's someone very keen to purchase and he has offered a ridiculously high price. Had I known that before, I could have outbid you for that guitar!'

'A guitar which I no longer possess,' he responded with an ironic twist of his lips. 'But what prompted you to go to that sale? Did you know the instrument belonged to Vancells?'

'Yes, my mother once spoke of it, told me it had been stolen. Then Jaume wrote to her, suggesting it may be in London and begged her to keep an eye on the catalogues in case it should be offered for sale. Of course, I didn't expect it to fetch fifteen thousand, nor had I the capital to stay in the bidding.'

'And now it appears to have been stolen a second time,' he remarked with a sigh.

The ring of the telephone broke into their conversation.

Immediately she picked up the receiver a heavily accented voice asked, 'Señorita, where is the package Pujol gave you?'

'Where is the what? I don't understand— who are you?'

'Do not play games with me. Pujol gave you something at the airport. Where is it?'

Almost speechless with shock, she managed to repeat, 'Who are you?'

'If you do not tell me,' the caller snarled, 'it will not be the housekeeper who suffers, it will be you!'

Fiona dropped the receiver with a crash, her mind reeling as she turned to meet Rafel's expression of concern.

'Something is wrong?' he asked. 'You have bad news?'

Wordlessly, she nodded, then gasped, 'It's so frightening!'

'Tell me what is troubling you. Maybe I can help,' he offered, gently propelling her towards a chair.

Comforted by his presence, she stifled her fear and let her hand remain in his as she related the caller's threats.

*   *   *

Rafel drove home deep in thought. A connection between his experience at the airport and the break-in at the Vancells' villa had confirmed Ferrer's suspicions. When he had arrived at the villa, the inspector had scratched his balding head and, after staring out on to the terrace for some time, decided he would continue surveillance on the villa and have the telephone tapped in the event of further calls.

'Obviously, they expected to find what they wanted in your room, senyorita,' Ferrer had concluded earlier. 'But although you both state no such package exchanged hands, I think we can safely assume further attempts will be made.'

What package was the caller referring to, Rafel asked himself repeatedly throughout his journey back to Barcelona. But the only satisfaction he gained was that he now knew for certain the girl was innocent. She had become involved in something far deeper than even he at first had been aware, something from which he must ensure she was protected.

He recalled how, only a short time before, she had trembled in his arms as they waited for the inspector. He'd experienced a wild desire to blank the disturbing situation from his mind and kiss her perfectly moulded lips. And when Ferrer recovered from his astonishment over finding them together, he'd been none too pleased to learn her involvement in the incident at the airport had been withheld. His expression was grave as he declared his intention to visit Rafel the following day.

*　　　*　　　*

Rafel slept restlessly that night, the events of the day cascading through his mind, so that by the time the inspector called next morning, he was in a rather tetchy mood. Ferrer entered the study carrying a large brown paper parcel, which he unwrapped with a triumphant flourish.

'Your property, I believe, Professor,' he said, a smug expression on his round face. 'Naturally, I regret it is broken, but feel my department ought to be congratulated on its efficiency!'

Uttering an exclamation of extreme dismay, Rafel stared down at the once beautiful rosewood guitar, the wood splintered where the soundboard had been partly wrenched from its polished body.

'How could anyone do this?' he exploded. 'Where did you find it, Inspector?'

'Beside the road leading from the airport,' he said as Rafel cursed afresh. 'It is yours? You can identify it?'

'Of course. Did I not give you the maker's name, and the year? Perhaps it has not occurred to you, Inspector, this is the work of vandals, not thieves!'

'I disagree, and it would have helped if you had been frank with me regarding Señorita Maxwell in the first place,' Ferrer returned dryly as he drew his heavy frame to full height, assuming a little more superiority.

Rafel glanced up from the desk to meet the inspector's implacable expression. 'Forgive me, but my disappointment is so great, I could kill whoever did this terrible thing!' he declared passionately, examining the guitar with a tenderness Ferrer couldn't appreciate. 'Even so, I'm grateful for its return, whatever the condition.'

The inspector leaded over the desk.

'But the matter is not yet closed, Señor. You may be satisfied with the return of your precious instrument, I am not! It is my opinion they expected to find what they wanted

49

concealed inside but it had already been removed. Also, there is now the telephone call to Señorita Maxwell to consider. Tell me, what was it you gave her at the airport?'

Rafel's head shot up.

'Really! We have been over all that.'

'You withheld information from me at the outset.'

'I gave the girl nothing. Believe me, that is the truth.'

Ferrer sighed, thoughtful for a moment before he asked, 'What do you know about the Maxwell girl? Does she have friends here?'

'Friends?' Rafel's dark eyes narrowed. 'What possible connection would they have with this case?'

Ferrer tapped a thick forefinger on his chin.

'Merely curiosity,' he replied, reaching for his briefcase as he went on to say, 'Incidentally, we checked the guitar for fingerprints, though should we uncover the culprit I'll deal with him. I want no further threats of violence from you.'

Rafel shot him an indignant look, but caught a twinkle in Ferrer's eyes as he turned to add, 'Meanwhile, enjoy your friendship with Señorita Maxwell. She is an extremely attractive young woman.'

*   *   *

Señora Pujol entered the study to find her son

50

at his desk, gazing down on the broken guitar, his expression a mixture of anger and dismay.

'Surely, this is not the valuable instrument you spoke of,' she began. 'Did the inspector bring it here?'

'Si, just look at it!' he snapped, flicking the neck which dangled on a single string.

'You ought to have taken more care and carried it as hand luggage.'

'Really, Mama, do you imagine the authorities would consider a packing case almost twice that size as hand luggage!'

Catching her hurt expression he murmured an apology and explained, 'I've decided to take it to the makers for advice. I am free of lectures tomorrow so it is a good opportunity.'

'I understand,' she said with an indulgent smile. 'Let us hope it can be repaired to your satisfaction.'

Rafel re-wrapped the guitar and looked out to where his car was parked beneath the trees. The instrument was back in his possession, but he still felt uneasy. What exactly had the thief been looking for? Before the sale he had inspected it closely. Had anything been secreted inside he felt sure it would have affected the quality of its tone.

He considered inviting Fiona to accompany him on the drive to the repairer whose workshop stood some forty kilometres to the south. She had lingered in his thoughts throughout most of the night, and now he experienced a longing to meet her again.

He quickly placed a call to the villa.

*   *   *

Following the call from Rafel, Fiona received another, this time from Mr Grey, requesting a meeting. He sounded annoyed when she told him of her intention to go out with Rafel Pujol.

'Do you think it wise? You hardly know the man, and I understood you to say there were more urgent matters you wished to discuss with me.'

'Sorry, he's already on his way here,' she said, experiencing a tremor of excitement at the prospect of seeing Rafel. 'In any case, you told me you were leaving for England.'

'Oh, very well,' Grey replied when she detected a note of annoyance in his voice, 'but maybe you could use this opportunity to discover what Pujol is concealing from the inspector. He may be involved in something illegal.'

'As I told you, Rafel Pujol is as mystified as I,' she said. 'However, if you give me your number, I'll call you tomorrow.'

'Not sure which office I'll be using so I will ring you.'

*   *   *

'Did you know this man Grey previous to your visit?' Rafel asked as he held open the door of his car.

'No, and he's not someone I care for. I find his manner rather strange, yet he showed a curiously protective attitude when I mentioned you were calling today.'

'Perhaps he doesn't trust me in the company of a pretty young lady.'

'And should I heed his judgement?' she countered, smiling.

A gleam of amusement entered his dark eyes.

'You're safe,' he assured her as they left the pine-fringed road to skirt the rocky coastline. 'Well, safe from whoever made that phone call two days ago. Incidentally, what is the name of the firm of solicitors employing Grey?'

Fiona shook her head.

'Strange as it may seem, I haven't been able to find that letter since my room was ransacked.'

'I expect it will turn up,' he said, then fell silent when the road narrowed, curving dangerously as the Mediterranean came into view.

'So beautiful,' Fiona murmured, releasing her breath slowly as the road straightened again.

'I always enjoy this drive. I've been visiting my old house in the country since I was a boy, when many city dwellers had such a weekend retreat. It is rather rustic, but so peaceful I can work on my lectures without interruption.'

He slowed as they reached the village of Garraf tucked away behind the rocky cliff face.

'Tell me, did you fly over especially to purchase the guitar?' she asked.

'Yes, plus some other business. Also, I visited an acquaintance with whom I attended a concert in the Albert Hall.'

'A lady?'

'No, no, a male friend from university days . . .'

'And he gave you a package to bring back to Barcelona?' she intervened smartly, watching closely for his reaction.

Compressing his lips, he drew the car to a halt and turned to face her.

'Exactly what do you mean by that?' he grated and saw her colour rise. 'I thought I had convinced you no such package exists!'

'Be honest with me,' she pleaded, shaking her head. 'There must be a package, otherwise why the phone call?'

'Quite frankly, I have no idea. I can appreciate why you ask and I feel responsible for the fact you have become involved.'

'But there must be a reason!' she cried, her eyes flashing. 'And as I am involved, why won't you tell me?'

'Fiona, listen to me,' he demanded, taking her by the shoulders. 'You must accept my word. After all, I accepted your reason for my name being on your list.'

'So, you didn't believe me. You accepted it but . . .'

'Ai!' he exclaimed in exasperation. 'We must trust each other. Nothing will be solved this way.'

Uttering a sigh of resignation she nodded.

'Perhaps you are right, but you must realise the unnerving effect this has had on me. I didn't sleep a wink last night.'

His hands slid from her shoulders during seconds of silent scrutiny.

'Si, I do, but I won't let anything happen to you, and Ferrer promised he would send a man to the villa.'

'Yes, I saw a fellow on the patio earlier, but I don't know if he's there all the time.'

'All the more reason why you should spend more time with me, then I can ensure you come to no harm. Come, let us drive on, there is a wonderful museum in Sitges. If we hurry we should reach it before it closes for the afternoon.'

'Siesta time,' she murmured, relaxing after his assurances.

'Si, but in the Catalan language it is *sesta*, also time for eating. I know an hotel where the food can be recommended.'

After parking the car on the road beside the promenade, they mounted the flight of steps leading up to the church. From their elevated position they looked out over the calm sea, unaware of the dark saloon which had come to a halt below. Along a narrow, cobbled street behind the church stood the Cau Ferrat Museum where Rafel pointed out the many works of Rusiñol which, he told her, means Nightingale in English.

'Oh, what a lovely name.'

'Yes. He was a Catalan artist who gave his name to the town,' he continued, oblivious to the fact that his movements were being observed from the doorway.

Ascending the narrow stairs to reach the floor above, he saw her look of surprise as they confronted an early oil by Picasso, and was moved by her tender expression as she gazed at a painting of Saint Peter by El Greco and murmured, 'I'm so pleased you brought me here.'

'I hope you will allow me to take you on a further tour as we possess a wealth of art and culture here. One moment, let me take your hand,' he advised as they made to descend the steep stairs, but as they went down, her hand suddenly tightened on his.

'Rafel,' she whispered, 'that man near the exit. Do you know him?'

'He followed her eyes to the figure below who quickly disappeared through the open doorway.

'I don't think so,' he replied. 'Why do you ask?'

'He seemed to be staring at us.'

'It's a common habit. Take it as a compliment. After all, it is not every day that a man sees such a pretty girl!' he exclaimed softly.

'Maybe I'm being over dramatic.'

She laughed, wrinkling her nose at him in an evocative way, and allowed her hand to remain in his as they left the museum to walk in the direction of the Tropic hotel where they dawdled over a late lunch. During the meal, Rafel reconsidered her earlier observation. Had the man been watching them, or merely admiring Fiona's fair beauty? Perhaps he also was in danger of becoming over dramatic, yet he found the thought rather disturbing.

It was four-thirty by the time they reached the little workshop of the instrument maker but found the door to be closed.

'He will be in no hurry to open,' Rafel said on his return to the car. 'We may as well relax until he appears.'

When the workshop eventually opened, he took the parcel from the boot and led the way inside. Fiona was fascinated by the collection of stringed instruments hanging from the whitewashed ceiling, some past repair and thick with lacy cobwebs but treasured by the owner of the business, Señor Sesrovires.

'Professor!' the man exclaimed, clasping Rafel by the hand. 'What a surprise!'

'A surprise indeed, though I would have preferred this to be a social visit,' Rafel replied, opening the parcel to reveal the damaged guitar. 'What can you make of this?'

Señor Sesrovires' expression of pleasure quickly faded as he regarded the shattered contents.

'Ai, ai!' he exclaimed, shaking his head in dismay. 'Terrible!'

'You will work on it?' Rafel asked hopefully. 'It is one of your grandfather's, one he made for Vancells' father.'

'Si, si, Professor, but to repair it . . .' He blew out his cheeks and continued, 'It would be easier to make one!'

'Ah, no, this one is too precious, it must be repaired. I brought it back from England only last week.'

'And it is my guess you paid a handsome sum for it. Was there much competition?'

'Not really. The price rose too high for most bidders.'

The man gave a knowing smile.

'Sentimentalist, eh? The elder Vancells gave you lessons, did he not?'

Rafel nodded.

'Will you call me when it is ready?'

'Si, but it may take a while. I have much work here.'

'Thank you, I will wait. Adieu.'

*   *   *

'Fiona, there is something I have been

58

meaning to ask you,' Rafel said as they returned to his car. 'Can you recollect the man who bid against me after you dropped out?'

'Not clearly. He was seated some distance away and, if you remember, I left when it looked hopeless for me.'

'I didn't get a clear view of him though, by his appearance, I guessed him to be a fellow countryman. I noticed he gave up when the bidding reached nearly three million pesetas.'

'Probably felt as I did, hopelessly beaten,' she reminded him woefully. 'I never dreamed it would fetch such a sum!'

Shooting her a rueful smile he settled down to a steady pace at the wheel. Again he wondered what had driven the bidding to such heights. Only a sentimental longing to possess the Vancells guitar had urged him to continue to bid higher than originally planned. He recalled Sesrovires' figures—half a million pesetas. Had it been merely guesswork on his part?

Retracing their route through Sitges, they began to climb the hazardous cliff road when Fiona gasped as she saw the narrow verge fell steeply away to the sea below. But he drove with care, resisting the temptation to give full throttle to his powerful car, keeping the following vehicle impatiently close on his tail. Nearing a particularly steep curve, he dropped into a low gear and relaxed until, in the rear view mirror, he glimpsed the car behind pulling out to overtake as they neared the fast approaching bend.

'Oh, no!' he exclaimed, 'the fool is going to . . .'

He paused, suddenly realising the other car was far too close as it came alongside and began to cut across their path, closing in on the offside wing.

Instantly, he slammed on the brakes and pulled on the wheel before he flung a protective arm in front of Fiona. Her cry of alarm was muffled by the screech of tyres as the rear of the car skidded sideways on the loose gravel of the verge. A fresh curse exploded from his lips as the other car accelerated away with a squeal of rubber as it took the bend.

'The fool! The crazy fool!' he ranted, easing the car off the narrow verge.

'I thought we were going over the side,' she gasped through trembling lips. 'If you hadn't pulled up so quickly . . .'

'Pity I didn't get his number. I was too concerned with . . . hey, you're shaking! Are you hurt?'

She shook her head, relieved to be back on the hard surface.

'The seatbelt saved me from lurching forward.'

'We couldn't catch him now, so I propose to take you home. I'm sorry the outing ended this way, Fiona. You must have been terrified.'

She managed a brave smile.

'After the way you handled this car I would never criticise your driving.'

He grinned and cast her a sideways glance, then drove along in silence, depressed by the thought of returning her to the villa so early. But his spirits lifted when he helped her alight from the car and she invited him indoors.

'Tea and cakes,' she said, 'do they appeal to you? Rather late for afternoon tea, I know.'

He smiled.

'Thank you, I was hoping you would invite me.'

'Actually, I had another motive for asking,' she admitted. 'Rosa is visiting her sister. I shall feel more relaxed if you can stay until she returns.'

'Of course. I wouldn't consider leaving you alone.'

Over tea they chatted for almost two hours. Rafel was considering inviting her out to dinner when the telephone rang.

'Probably Rosa,' Fiona said. 'She worries about me.'

'I am pleased to hear that,' he began, but knew immediately it was not Rosa when he saw the expression on Fiona's face.

Moving quickly to her side he covered her hand on the receiver and leaned closer.

'Yes, Señorita,' he heard, 'this time you escaped the accident, but perhaps it will convince you we mean business. Next time you will not be so fortunate, unless you will speak now.'

Rafel nodded, encouraging her to reply.

'What do you want to know?' she managed. 'Who are you?'

'The small package, Señorita, where is it?'

'I haven't got a pack . . .' she began shakily but, unable to bear her distress, Rafel took the receiver.

'There is no package,' he stated harshly, 'and if you have anything more to say, you deal with me!'

'Persuade her to co-operate, Señor,' the caller hissed. 'But if you involve the police, her next accident will be fatal!'

Before Rafel could respond, he realised the line was dead.

'I shall phone the inspector,' he said as she sank down on a chair. 'I can not bear to see you so distressed.'

'I'm not going to allow that man to intimidate me!' she declared. 'After that incident with the car I know you have no knowledge of what he's after.'

CHAPTER 4

'I understand they haven't been able to trace that call,' Rafel said, meeting Fiona's anxious gaze. 'Also, Ferrer's short of manpower so he has arranged for the officer on this beat to keep an eye on the place tonight. If you wish, I'll stay until he arrives.'

It was gathering dusk when he went out to collect something from his car. As he crossed the terrace a figure stepped from the shadows of the creeper-laden pillars. Rafel hesitated then, in his own tongue, challenged the newcomer.

'It was the officer on duty in this area,' he told Fiona when he returned indoors. 'He's taking a look around. He will be back later, but take care.'

'I'm not being very hospitable after you stayed so long,' she said. 'You must have a meal before you go.'

In the kitchen, Fiona set out plates of meat and salad and pieces of crusty bread and this, together with a carafe of wine, made a satisfying meal. After they had eaten, the officer on duty came to advise Fiona to secure all windows and doors before he contacted his superior on his carphone.

'And the inspector will call tomorrow,' Rafel continued to translate in response to Fiona's enquiring glance.

Shortly afterwards, when Rosa bustled in, Rafel decided it was time for him to leave.

'Now Rosa is here I'll lock up and go to my room,' Fiona said as she accompanied him to the door. 'I didn't sleep at all well last night.'

'I understand, you must be tired. I trust we shall meet again?' he ended.

'Yes. I may be in Barcelona tomorrow—you know, about selling this place. I should get a call in the morning.'

'Unfortunately, I have lectures, but I advise you not to make a hasty decision. After what you told me, Fiona, there's something about that agent that is not quite right, and you may not want to sell. I hope you don't.'

He gave a quick smile and offered her his mobile phone. 'Take this, I have another. Ring me, will you?'

*   *   *

From inside his car, Rafel saw a light go on in an upstairs window. Turning the key in the ignition, he drove a short distance along the road before pulling on to the verge between the trees and switching off the lights. Sitting in almost total darkness, with the window down, he kept an eye on the road behind in the interior mirror and listened for the sound of anyone approaching the villa now the officer had driven away. Since the incident with the car, he'd felt uneasy, and the ensuing threat over the telephone had increased his anxiety. He was reluctant to leave for home.

For two hours he kept a watch on the place, wishing he could be with Fiona. His emotions surprised him. How soon he had become protective towards this beautiful English girl. And as he continued to watch, he fantasised about his feelings for her until he fell into a warm doze.

*   *   *

It was early the following morning when Rafel turned the key in the lock of his home. The street was still. Only the first awakening song of birds in the nearby trees and the hum of distant traffic reached his ears as he slipped in and went up to his room to ponder over the events of the previous day.

It had been the sound of the local policeman's engine that had aroused him from sleep in the car. As he'd eased his cramped muscles, he had been thankful to see it turn in front of the villa, leaving him unnoticed as it went off in the opposite direction. Soon after that, he left, and now he dozed in a chair, only waking in time to join his mother at breakfast.

She greeted him with an expression of undisguised annoyance.

'I do wish you would tell me when you intend to be late!' she said crossly. 'Someone called here during the evening, around seven-thirty, and asked for you.'

'Who was it? What did he want?'

'He wished to see some of your books, and when I told him you were not at home, he insisted you had given him permission to enter your study and help himself.'

'Help himself!' Rafel echoed. 'Certainly not! Did he give his name?'

'No, he didn't disclose any details about himself. I haven't seen him before. He was not one of your university colleagues, so I suggested he should call again, when you are at home.'

'Strange,' Rafel murmured, 'not giving his name.'

'I thought so, too, so when he became quite persistent I called for José and we threatened him with the police. Somehow, I didn't trust the man.'

'What did he look like, Mama? Can you describe him?'

The Señora screwed up her mouth and replied thoughtfully, 'He was young, early twenties perhaps. Dark and bearded—spoke with a slight accent, but he is not Catalan. Ah, yes, part of one finger was missing.'

'Graçias, Mama, you are most observant. I'm pleased you refused to allow him into the house.'

'Many of your books are valuable, I know. You are careful to whom you lend them.'

'You're wonderful!' he exclaimed, planting a swift kiss on her cheek. 'My own little private eye!'

*   *   *

Inspector Ferrer did not expect to be called quite so early that morning, so when the telephone at his bedside roused him from a heavy slumber he responded irritably to the officer on duty at Castelldefels. Soon after his arrival at the villa, as he was discussing events with the local officer, Fiona came out on the terrace.

'Good morning, gentlemen,' she said. 'I didn't expect to see you so early in the day. Is everything all right?'

The younger of the two men cast her an admiring glance, whereas the inspector's expression was solemn as he advanced her way.

'Were you aware of anyone out here during the night, Señorita? Did you have a visitor? Were you disturbed?'

'No to all three questions, Inspector. Why, was someone here?'

'You tell me. The matter can then be solved.'

Puzzled, she queried, 'Tell you, Inspector? Tell you what?'

'At what time did Señor Pujol leave?'

She frowned. 'Around nine o'clock, I think,

or soon after. Why do you ask? He's all right, isn't he?'

'Si, si, but did he return after midnight?'

'Certainly not, well not to my knowledge, but from that I assume someone else was here.'

'This area is part of the officers beat, and at three this morning he observed a car pulling off the verge as he was travelling in the other direction. He was unable to describe the vehicle accurately, though I understand it was like that of Señor Pujol. It drove off at high speed.'

'I'm sure he can verify his time of departure, Inspector. Sorry, I can't be of more help,' she said as she turned to go indoors.

'Rosa, did anyone telephone whilst I was outside talking to the inspector?' she asked the housekeeper.

'No, Señorita, I would have called you.'

'Mr Grey promise to arrange for me to call at his office in Barcelona. I expected him to ring before now. He wants to know what I intend to do about this house, but perhaps he's not yet back from England.'

Rosa clicked her tongue.

'Not very businesslike, this man. But you will stay here?'

Fiona smiled.

'You're the second person to ask me that. I do like it, but I'm not sure.'

'I think the Señor professor is the other

person,' Rosa said, barely suppressing a giggle.

Fiona sent her an amused glance.

'Maybe, Rosa, but I want an end to the trouble here before I decide.'

There was no call from Herbert Grey that morning. By lunchtime Fiona had given up the idea of going to Barcelona and was having a quiet afternoon in the garden, until the mobile telephone rang, causing her a surge of pleasure when she heard Rafel's voice.

'So, you haven't been to Barcelona?' he guessed.

'No, I haven't heard from Mr Grey.'

'Ah, well, perhaps tomorrow,' he said, then continued, 'Ferrer has been to see me, and I understand he was enquiring what time I left yesterday evening.'

'Yes, and he wanted to know if you came back later,' she broke in. 'Something about a car that may have been yours.'

'It was mine,' he confessed with chuckle. 'Actually, I stayed out there for a while, just to make sure the policeman did his rounds as promised, but I fell asleep.'

'Fell asleep!' she echoed laughingly. 'What time was that?'

'Not sure, well after midnight, I think. I was concerned about you, wanted to be sure all was well before I left.'

'Oh, Rafel, you are thoughtful. I had locked and bolted the doors as promised but, even so, it was a creepy feeling to think someone might be out there.'

He laughed. 'And guess who it was! At least you have Rosa for company.'

'Yes but I don't want to worry her unnecessarily.'

'Well, now you have the mobile, you can call me whenever you wish. I'll look forward to hearing from you.'

'I'll keep it with me all the time, indoors or out.'

'Please, Fiona, be careful if you go outside. I have no desire to worry you, but our troubles may not be over.'

By late afternoon, Fiona was beginning to wonder how long she should wait for Herbert Grey to contact her. He'd been so evasive about his movements she was beginning to feel there was something behind the suspicions of both Rosa and Rafel.

'How did Mr Grey know what flight I was taking, and the time of my arrival?' she asked Rosa as they sorted through her uncles' sheet music.

'I first see this man on the day of the funeral. He was speaking with a student of your late uncle and I hear him speak about you coming here. Then this man, Grey, insists he will meet you,' Rosa continued agitatedly. 'He asks me what time you are arriving.'

Their conversation was cut short by the ring of the mobile phone. To Fiona's delight it was Rafel, and when he suggested he drive over for

70

the evening, she invited him to dinner.

'Rosa, can you help me prepare for a guest this evening?' she asked once he'd rung off. 'I'd like to do something special but I'm not used to the appliances in this kitchen.'

'It is a pleasure. Maybe a casserole with rabbit and almonds in the bitter chocolate sauce, yes?'

'Mm, sounds wonderful, Rosa. I'll leave it to you.'

When Fiona descended the stairs in the early evening she was met by the pleasant aroma of cooking. She was looking forward to Rafel arriving and wanted everything to go well. A slight smile played on her lips as she glanced at her reflection in the hall mirror. Fresh from a shower, she had chosen to wear a dress in pastel shades, and high-heeled sandals. And, for a cool effect, she had swept up her hair in a cluster of loose curls on the crown of her head, aware the style suited her well.

'Ai, Señorita, you look very special tonight!' the housekeeper exclaimed when she joined her in the kitchen.

'Thank you, Rosa. Oh, what a delicious smell!' she exclaimed, lifting the casserole lid. 'You must give me the recipe.'

Fiona's expression brightened at the sound of a car, and she hurried towards the front door. Rafel's eyes slid over her admiringly as he stood in the open doorway.

'What a picture you make!' he exclaimed, producing a spray of long-stemmed red roses bound by silver ribbons. 'A beautiful flower for a beautiful lady.'

Her cheeks pink, she led him inside where they enjoyed an aperitif. The meal was a success, and the local wine accompanying it lifted Fiona's spirits, a temporary respite from the tension she had felt. They chatted at length over coffee and discussed the sheet music she had sorted, but when the time came for Rafel to leave she felt her nervousness return.

'We will lock the doors as the inspector said we should,' Rosa promised when Rafel wished her farewell.

'Indeed you should,' he said, smiling until he noticed Fiona's anxious expression.

Dropping a kiss on her cheek, he assured her, 'I don't think you need worry. The local police will take care of everything.'

*   *   *

Going to where his car was parked by the gate, Rafel paused and looked around. He'd heard the door bolts slide home after Fiona had promised she would not open it to anyone until the morning when she could view any callers from the window. And now he saw a light go on upstairs, but as he pulled away, he noticed it was from a balcony door of one of the bedrooms and it stood slightly ajar. He remembered Fiona saying she slept at the front of the house, yet he could see, for a reasonably agile man, reaching the balcony would not be difficult. He ought to warn her.

Driving along the road to where he had parked the previous evening, he pulled on to the verge and switched off the headlights. Taking his mobile phone from beneath the dashboard he dialled the number of the mobile he had given her, warmly anticipating the sound of her voice, until a recorded message told him it wasn't switched on.

With a groan of dismay, he looked back at the villa through the interior mirror and saw the light was still visible. So desperately had he wanted to comfort Fiona before he left, reassure her he'd do everything in his power to see she came to no harm, he now knew he had to go back. There was nothing else for it. He must bang on the front door hoping she would come down, or, he would climb up to the balcony himself!

Deciding to approach the villa on foot, he kept a watchful eye for the local policeman, realising his plan of entry would be difficult to explain. He moved quietly along the roadside, skirting the lawn to reach the cover of the shadows. Pausing to control his breathing, he listened for the sound of a police car. He scanned the wall to where the wrought-iron balcony ran along to the leaf-laden branches of the tree that grew by the end wall.

Treading softly, he moved towards the tree where, with one quick spring, he caught hold of the lower branches and hauled himself up within reach of the balcony. Taking a deep breath he reached forward to grab the rail, climbing over as silently as possible in case she became alarmed. Once on the other side, he flattened his body against the open shutters. He'd found the climb to the balcony quite easy.

Looking through a narrow opening in the heavy net drapes, the room appeared to be unoccupied. He spoke her name in a low voice, but the only sound he heard was the gurgle of running water. Repeating her name, he entered and crossed the tiled floor toward the bathroom and saw her back was turned in his direction. It seemed she hadn't heard, but before he could speak, she must have sensed his presence. She tensed suddenly and gave a sharp intake of breath.

'Ssh! It's me, Rafel,' he whispered, swiftly covering her mouth with his hand as he drew her back against him. 'Don't be frightened.'

Her struggling ceased, and as she relaxed he released his grip.

'How did you get in?' she gasped. 'Did Rosa open the door?'

'No, no, I came by way of the balcony,' he explained. 'I didn't intend to alarm you, but I thought you may have screamed until you saw who it was.'

'You're right, I would!' she said agitatedly. 'You gave me quite a scare.'

'I'm sorry, but you really should have locked the balcony door. I saw it was ajar. I could have been just anyone.'

'I know, but it's so warm,' she protested, drawing her towelling robe tightly around her. 'I can't sleep with the doors closed.'

'Then I suggest you keep the outer shutters locked in future,' he advised. 'The internal doors, too, if you can bear it. I must confess, secretly I'm glad you didn't. I just had to come back, make sure you are safe. If you like, I'll check the locks work,' he said, switching off the lights before going to close the shutters and turn the key.

'It was thoughtful of you to come back,' she whispered as he returned to her side. 'I'm sorry I snapped.'

'No, no, it is understandable. It is unfortunate you should have become involved in this awful business, but I am quite sure the inspector will soon put an end to it.'

'Oh, Rafel, I do hope so, for your sake as well as mine, then you won't need to worry about me any more.'

'Does that mean you wish to dismiss me from your life?' he queried. 'I had hoped our friendship would continue.'

'Oh no,' she assured him with a quick smile. 'Anyway, you promised to show me around

Barcelona, remember?'

He chuckled quietly and reached out in a spontaneous gesture, taking her hands and drawing her towards him. For a split second he felt her resist, then she relaxed and moved into his arms, trembling slightly as he tightened his embrace, pressing her warm body against his own.

'I just had to come back,' he whispered. 'I hated leaving you alone.'

'I have Rosa,' she murmured, 'though I must admit I feel safer when you're around.'

'Ah, Fiona!' he exclaimed softly, looking down on her upturned face for a long, breathless moment before he sought her lips.

'Must I leave now?' he murmured as their lips drew slowly apart. 'Maybe you feel less anxious when I am here.'

She uttered a shuddering sigh.

'Oh, yes, I feel much safer but I don't think I know you well enough to ask you to stay.'

He suppressed a smile as he glanced across to the easy chair.

'If you wish, I'll stay with you until daylight. That chair will do nicely.'

*　　　*　　　*

It was almost five o'clock the following morning when Rafel arrived home. Going immediately to his room, he lay on the bed staring thoughtfully at the ceiling. Fiona had

76

been comforted by his presence. She had called him when something awakened her, and he had gone willingly to her side. He now realised he was growing increasingly fond of the girl.

As dawn broke, convinced Rosa would see him, Fiona had persuaded him to leave, promising to switch on her phone and lock the balcony doors behind him. The man on duty had been nowhere in sight as he retreated swiftly by the way he had entered and returned to his car.

Now, in a state of happy reverie, he felt his eyelids close, allowing him to drift into a contented sleep. But it seemed as though only minutes had passed when he woke to the ringing of the telephone by his bed. He glanced at the clock and grimaced. A quarter past six—it wouldn't be Fiona. She would use the mobile.

It was Ferrer's cool, authorative voice that came over the line, demanding to know where he had spent the night.

'Here, Inspector, of course,' he said convincingly. 'Why do you ask?'

'Did you visit Señorita Maxwell last evening?'

'Yes, I had dinner at the villa.'

'At what time did you leave?' Ferrer pressed.

There was a slight hesitation before Rafel replied. 'It would be around ten-thirty, I believe, what is this about?'

'But you didn't return immediately to Barcelona,' the inspector said and continued coldly, 'Perhaps you went a little further south to visit your friend Sesrovires and see what progress he is making with the guitar.'

'No, Inspector, I have not seen Sesrovires since I first took the instrument for repair.'

'Then someone else is more interested in his progress than you, Professor. Sesrovires was discovered semi-conscious in his workshop in the early hours of this morning!'

CHAPTER 5

Ferrer moved quickly. By eight forty-five he had Rafel at the station and now faced him across a bare table in the interrogation room.

'You say you left the Vancells' villa at around ten-thirty last night?' he repeated, trailing a thick forefinger down his notes.

'Si, si. The Señorita was tired. She has not be sleeping well,' Rafel submitted. 'No doubt she will confirm my statement.'

'I am asking you, Professor! Also, there is the housekeeper. Can she confirm the time?'

'Of course, she was there when I left.'

'As Señorita Maxwell is so nervous and losing sleep,' Ferrer broke in, 'could it be, perhaps, that you returned to comfort her?'

'No, no, Inspector, I drove straight home.'

'Your mother stated it was much later when you arrived.'

Rafel shrugged. 'Look, Inspector,' he began, 'I know nothing of Sesrovires' unfortunate accident.'

'Accident, Señor? This was no accident, I assure you.'

'Whatever it was, I am not responsible. I like the man so why would I show violence towards him?'

'But you have threatened to kill—I heard you myself—and the guitar was not in

79

Sesrovires' workshop.'

'If I had been serious, was I likely to inform you of my intentions? I was extremely angry over the destruction of my guitar, but I couldn't kill anyone!'

'I realise you are passionately fond of musical instruments, but to commit murder for such an object does seem out of character.'

'Si, si, most definitely, Inspector, believe me!'

Ferrer regarded him thoughtfully a moment before he asked, 'Tell me, Professor, are you also passionately fond of the Señorita Maxwell?'

Rafel glanced up to reply cautiously, 'She is a very becoming young woman.'

'So becoming you could not resist the desire to return to the villa?' he put in smartly, and when Rafel merely stared in silence, he went on, 'Never mind, we'll come back to that later. But unless you can provide me with a sound alibi to cover your movements during the early hours, I have no alternative but to hold you whilst we investigate further.'

*   *   *

Fiona was seated in the garden with Rosa, a large parasol protecting them from the late morning sun, when she heard footsteps coming along the path. Immediately, her fingers tightened on the mobile phone beside her until she spotted Inspector Ferrer cutting across the lawn.

'Good day, Señorita, Señora,' he began politely before directing his attention to Fiona. 'I wish to discuss a certain matter with you, Miss Maxwell, I trust this is a convenient time?'

Rosa got to her feet.

'Shall I bring coffee, Señorita?'

Fiona nodded and indicated Ferrer should take the vacant chair.

'Good morning, Inspector, what is it you wish to discuss?'

Ferrer loosened his jacket and reached into the pocket for his notes.

'You have no more telephone calls, no unwelcome visitors?' he began, and when she shook her head, continued, 'And now, regarding the professor, what time did he leave here last night?'

Nervous under the close scrutiny, Fiona felt her cheeks grow warm.

'Oh, sometime after dinner, I'm not quite sure,' she replied, glancing away as Rosa approached with a tray.

Ferrer waited until Rosa had withdrawn, accepting the cup of coffee Fiona poured before he continued.

'The professor tells me it would be about ten-thirty. This is so?'

'Yes, he could be right,' she agreed quickly, 'and Rosa can verify that. She saw him leave.

Why do you ask?'

'Mm, that could be,' Ferrer murmured, reaching for the sugar. 'You English dine much earlier, whereas here, it could be midnight before we finish our meal.'

Engrossed in his notes, Ferrer drank quickly, and rather noisily, she thought. But when the silence became almost unbearable, she ventured, 'More coffee, Inspector, or was there something else?'

'Are you aware of the disturbance at the house of Señor Sesrovires, the instrument maker?' he queried, holding her in a questioning gaze. 'I believe you accompanied the professor there recently.'

'I met him, yes. Why, what has happened?'

'According to his wife, the poor man was attacked around one o'clock this morning. He was in a state of near unconsciousness when we reached him.'

'Oh, how awful!' she exclaimed. 'I do hope he recovers. Does the professor know? He'll be most upset.'

'We discussed it earlier.' Ferrer told her. 'And now we are holding him at the station on suspicion of being involved in this incident.'

'But that's impossible!' she gasped. 'He wouldn't have had the time.'

'Would not have had the time, Señorita? Exactly what does that mean?'

'But surely you don't think he's responsible?' she blurted out. 'He wouldn't do anything like that!'

'He is unable to account for his movements during the night,' Ferrer stated. 'And you have not answered my question. What was it you meant about time?'

'He was here, with me,' she began hesitantly.

'He came back to the house in the night?'

'No,' she replied in a small voice, 'he didn't actually leave. That is how I know it couldn't be Rafel.'

'Yet, you say the housekeeper saw him leave. So, what time did he return, and why?'

'He came back to tell me to lock my bedroom door.'

'Ah! But how did he know it was unlocked if he had already left the house?' he continued shrewdly. 'Did you answer the door to him, or was it the housekeeper?'

'No, I mean the outside balcony door, which is the way he came in,' she said quietly, glancing down at her clasped hands. 'You see, he had seen a gap of light as he drove away and was worried someone may get in.'

Ferrer stifled a smile as he returned, 'And he did!'

'Yes, it was fortunate he noted it.'

'Fortunate indeed! How long did he stay?'

'Oh, er, until about four, or maybe half-past,' she replied waveringly, and hurried on to explain. 'You see, we were talking, and listening to music.'

'Talking, listening to music?' Ferrer echoed, his brows raised. 'Were you not concerned about disturbing anyone?'

'It was turned low and we whispered,' she supplied uncomfortably. 'I didn't want to upset Rosa.'

'You whispered until four o'clock!' he exclaimed with an expression of faint amusement.

'Very well, Inspector, we kissed one or twice, but it went no further, if that's what you're thinking!' she cried indignantly, unable to endure his constant probing. 'Perhaps now you'll believe me.'

Seeing her heightened colour and flashing eyes, he touched her arm in a gesture of apology.

'Forgive me for goading you to make such a confession, but this I can believe.'

Tears welled in her eyes and she stifled a sob.

'You really do believe me, Inspector? Rafel is innocent, I know.'

Ferrer shrugged his broad shoulders.

'Si, Señorita, I did notice evidence of entry to your balcony—foliage from the tree on the ground below. However, for the time being, the professor must remain at the station. I cannot say more than that.'

'But why?' she implored, her eyes now brimming with tears. 'I've admitted where he was.'

'I know,' he said kindly, 'and for the moment I prefer you keep our conversation to yourself, you understand?'

'Don't worry, I'd rather no-one knew. Rosa seems a little old-fashioned and I'd hate her to have the wrong impression.'

Ferrer smiled. 'The professor wouldn't admit to being in your room so, obviously, he has a high regard for your reputation.'

'Perhaps if he knows I've told you, he may . . . ?'

'Perhaps. Meanwhile, you must be patient, Señorita, and inform me immediately should anything unusual occur.'

*　　　*　　　*

Anxious and frustrated, Rafel paced the floor of the interrogation room. Ferrer's last words had left him expecting to be locked in one of the cells, not merely detained under the watchful eye of a junior officer.

Stroking his stubbly chin, he began to wonder if he should have confessed to returning to the villa last night, but if he did there was no witness to corroborate his story. And he was beginning to feel certain the attack on Sesrovires could have been connected with the guitar.

*　　　*　　　*

It was after midday when the inspector returned. In the meantime, Rafel had refused the coffee brought to him, but now gladly accepted a cup of the strong, dark liquid.

'So, Professor,' Ferrer began, seating himself opposite, his chair creaking under the strain, 'you decided not to take advantage of your alibi. Can you tell me why?'

In the act of raising the cup to his lips, Rafel paused.

'My alibi?' he queried cautiously. 'Has something occurred to convince you I am not the man you seek?'

'The Señorita and I have had a satisfactory chat, and I have a witness who noticed your car parked a short distance from the villa in the early hours of this morning. Do you deny you were with the Señorita during this time?'

'Did she tell you this?'

'Did you spend the night in her room?' Ferrer persisted.

Rafel gave a reluctant sigh. 'Si, though not the entire night. I left around four, but prefer no-one else knows.'

He felt certain he saw a humorous quirk on the inspector's lips as he leaned forward to say, 'Your secret is safe, but you needed that alibi!'

'I assumed you would disregard it as merely an excuse.'

'I would have preferred you to allow me to be the judge!' Ferrer declared sternly. 'No-one else can confirm your whereabouts, and it is unlikely you would invite a third party to be present when you were alone together, even for the sake of your alibi! No, Professor, this is not the end of the matter, by any means.'

'But what happens now, Inspector? Must I remain here?'

Ferrer pondered a moment, tapping his teaspoon on the saucer.

'I intend to release you,' he submitted finally. 'However, I do not wish to publicise your release so, for the time being you must not visit or telephone the villa.'

Reluctantly, Rafel agreed and stared moodily at Ferrer. At least he could contact Fiona on his mobile phone, he thought, and rose to follow Ferrer to his office.

'The Señorita will not be in any danger,' Ferrer was saying as they walked along the corridor, 'and I shall inform you when you may resume your visits.'

Once Rafel had been released, Ferrer returned to his office where he summoned two of his men, issuing them with strict orders to keep him informed of the movements of both the professor and Miss Maxwell.

'Do not allow them out of your sight the minute they step outside!' he growled. 'Is that clear?'

*　　　*　　　*

When the mobile phone rang that evening,

Fiona's heart leapt, but when she heard Rafel say the inspector had instructed him not to visit, her spirits sank.

'Also, I must not telephone you,' he said with a chuckle, 'which is one rule already broken.'

'I'm so pleased you have, otherwise I would have rung you,' she said on a determined note.

'I hoped you would say that, but I want to see you, Fiona. There is much to discuss,' he said, going on to relate all that had occurred earlier that day.

'At least we can communicate this way.'

'I prefer to see you. Ferrer doesn't know what he is asking when he makes these ridiculous rules, though he hasn't said you may not visit me. Will you do that?'

'Yes, I suppose I could travel to Barcelona by train, though I'm not familiar with the city.'

'Can you come tomorrow?'

'I expect so. What time do you suggest?'

'If you can tell me the approximate time of your arrival, I'll be at the station to meet you. The trains are frequent but I suggest you get out at the first stop when you reach the city, and I'll have the car waiting.'

'So, I'm going to have my tour of Barcelona after all,' she said lightly, happy at the prospect of seeing Rafel.

'And we'll have lunch together. I know a secluded place where there will be no inspector lurking.'

'I'll get the first train leaving here after ten-thirty, and make sure Rosa keeps the doors locked whilst I'm out.'

'Good! Ferrer assured me you were in no danger so I suspect he's got a man patrolling your area, but best to be on your guard. Should anything occur, ring me. Promise?'

'I promise, and I'll keep the phone by me all the time.'

'I wish I could change places with it,' he said, chuckling softly. 'I'd do anything to be close to you right now.'

'I'll be with you tomorrow, Rafel, so you don't have long to wait,' she said, smiling to herself as she closed the line, but she hardly had time to think about what he had said before the telephone in the hall began to ring.

'That was Mr Grey on the line,' she told Rosa later as they sat down to dinner. 'He wanted to see me tomorrow but I told him he couldn't expect me to change my plans at such short notice. Curiously, he now seems quite keen for me to leave, though I'll admit I'm in no hurry to sell.'

'Ah, this is wonderful news!' Rosa broke in to exclaim. 'I will be very happy if you stay,' and, with a twinkle in her eye, added, 'The professor, also.'

*   *   *

Rafel's spirits rose as he anticipated the next

morning. The fact that Fiona had agreed to meet him without hesitation pleased him. But now he must check on the progress of Señor Sesrovires, hoping the news would be good. He sighed as he went to his study. Since his purchase of the old guitar, so many people had become disturbingly involved. He was beginning to wish he'd never set eyes on it in the first instance. Yet, without its initial theft he would not have met Fiona.

He was relieved to learn from the wife of Sesrovires that her husband was recovering well. He didn't consider it to be the right moment to enquire about the guitar so planned to call on the instrument maker once he was well enough to receive visitors. Ferrer had suggested Sesrovires might have discovered why the guitar had been so eagerly sought after, which meant he, too, might soon learn the reason.

At breakfast the following morning, his mother mentioned lunch.

'I'm afraid not,' he replied. 'I'm lunching with a colleague.'

The Señora clicked her tongue in displeasure. 'Rafel, your routine is impossible to follow!'

'Change of curriculum,' he supplied quickly. 'Nothing for you to worry your dear little head about.'

Casting him an indulgent smile, she confessed, 'I know I shouldn't fuss, but it's time you were married, then your wife would be the one to endure your irregular timetable. I'm too old for all these changes.'

'Nonsense.' He laughed but now, thinking about it, he knew she could be right. The subject of marriage had crossed his mind more than once in the last twenty-four hours.

*   *   *

Fiona reached the station with only ten minutes to wait before the train hissed to a halt alongside the platform in the direction of Barcelona. The carriage was crowded with passengers, the heat of the compartment oppressive, and she just managed to keep her balance in the dense, chattering crowd until a gentleman offered her his seat.

She was relieved to reach the city and rose when the first station was announced. Once on the platform she had to fight her way through the throng of people waiting to board, regretting the fact, she hadn't thought to phone Rafel beforehand. Not wishing to waste a precious second she headed for the exit until someone barred her path.

'Rafel!' she cried delightedly, looking up into his smiling face as his arms went around her, almost lifting her off her feet.

'You are pleased to see me?' he asked laughingly as he set her down.

'Of course, though I could have had another

appointment if I hadn't promised to meet you.'

'Already you have another man in your life!' he cried in mock dismay, holding her at arms' length.

'Oh no,' she protested, 'just the agent, he rang.'

'Fiona, my dearest,' he murmured, drawing her close once more, 'we are going to spend the whole day together.'

He guided her towards the escalator, leaving behind the still heat of the station for the busy street outside. Once they were in the car he pulled away quickly. She turned to him, her mind full of questions.

First, she asked, 'When where you released?' then, 'Does the inspector believe you are innocent? Who do you suppose attacked the instrument maker?'

He replied to each one as he expertly manoeuvred the vehicle through the heavy traffic.

'I do hope the poor man recovers,' she continued, 'otherwise, where is it all going to end?'

He shook his head. 'My mother had a visitor the evening before last. Told her he was a colleague, wanted to borrow my books.'

'Is that not usual in your profession?'

'True, but for some reason she suspected this man was not who he claimed to be and, by strange coincidence, he was missing part of one finger.'

'Oh, Rafel!' she gasped, experiencing a fresh wave of horror. 'What does it mean?'

'It could mean our troubles are not yet over,' he declared solemnly. 'However, I mentioned it to Ferrer so let's hope he can trace the man.'

Fiona fell silent, turning this latest piece of information over in her mind as the car joined the circle of traffic in Plaça de España. The very thought of that fellow still being at large unnerved her, and when she felt Rafel's hand cover hers she had difficulty returning his comforting smile.

'We will take the road up to Montjuich,' he decided. 'The view from there is quite something, also we have lots to discuss before lunch.'

'Whatever you suggest,' she agreed as the car took the steep incline with ease, relaxing a little as they passed the great fountains where her gaze wandered over the majestic buildings, both old and new.

Along another stretch of road they came to a circle of eight carved stone figures poised in dance. 'Monument to the Sardana,' he said, 'a traditional dance in which you really should take part.'

She smiled and nodded as enthusiastically as her troubled mind would allow, and when he brought the car to a halt near a group of trees she tried her utmost to appear relaxed.

'This is only a modest mountain,' he told

her, pressing a button to slide back the roof, 'a mere two hundred or so metres high, but the views of the city and port are quite splendid.'

She watched in silence whilst he took off his light jacket and placed it on the rear seat. His air of calm authority comforted her.

'You mentioned another appointment,' he said, turning to face her. 'Is it connected with Grey?'

'Yes, and I had the impression he can't wait to be rid of me, though Ferrer insists I stay on here until he is agreeable for me to travel.'

'And do you wish to return to England?' Rafel queried, one dark brow raised. 'Is that what you want?'

'I don't know what to say. Grey has no right to push me, particularly when I can't get him to name a meeting place, or give me his phone number.'

'Fiona, that is not what I asked. Tell me, do you wish to go?' he persisted, tilting her chin with one finger to hold her in close regard, compelling her to reply.

'No Rafel,' she said softly, 'not now.'

'My precious,' he murmured enfolding her in his arms, 'it is what I hoped you would say.'

'But I wish Ferrer would change his mind. I get nervous when you're not around.'

'I know, but Ferrer demanded I should not publicise my freedom. You will not mention it?'

'Not if that is what he wants, but why?'

94

'I can't be sure. Perhaps he wants the man who called at my home to think I'm still in custody. I notice he has someone watching the house and it's my guess there's another at the villa.'

'There's a policeman watching you? Are you sure?'

'Si, but I had parked my car in the next street and I managed to escape the house when he wandered away to have a smoke.'

Fiona couldn't resist a smile, and as she relaxed against the headrest, his lips came down on hers, holding them captive in a lingering kiss.

'I wanted to be with you so much,' he whispered hoarsely as they drew apart. 'Ferrer has imposed rules with which I can't possibly comply. But even when this dreadful business is over, please don't even consider returning to England.'

'There's no good reason for me to go. I have no family ties. I'd rather stay here with you,' she added softly before his lips silenced her again and she felt the immeasurable pleasure of his warm fingers lightly caressing her neck.

After a long, lazy lunch in a quiet country restaurant, the afternoon quickly passed into evening. It was growing dark by the time they drove back to the city. After parking the car, they strolled hand in hand in the still, warm air, along the Rambla, a wide avenue lined with plane trees, the central walkway thronged with people. Farther along they turned into a narrow street where men and women lounged in the doorways of numerous bars.

'Here we are,' he said as they drew near to a corner building where chicken roasted on a spit set into the outside wall. 'This is the restaurant Los Caracoles—to translate, The Snails!'

Fiona grimaced. 'Do they actually serve them here?'

'Si, also a range of traditional Catalan dishes. Care to try?'

A trifle apprehensively, she agreed and they followed the head waiter past an open kitchen where a fascinating assortment of fish and meat was being cooked on the large hotplate. Up a narrow staircase, the waiter preceded them through the rambling restaurant, coming to a halt at the table by a balcony that partly overlooked the busy kitchen below.

'It's a most unusual place,' Fiona remarked, looking down on the shelves laden with bottles of colourful liqueurs and huge, sherry-filled barrels beneath.

'And very popular,' he said, gesturing towards the crowded tables downstairs. 'Shall I translate the menu?'

'Anything but snails!' she exclaimed, laughing.

'Ah, but have you noticed the rolls?' he chuckled. 'They also are in the shape of a snail.'

'Then I have no choice,' she countered humorously, breaking a morsel from the brown crusty whirl on her plate.

He smiled and reached for her hand.

'It's wonderful to see you so happy, Fiona,' he said softly, and as his eyes rested upon her there came the sound of guitars and it was not long before a group of players paused by their table and a singer broke into a romantic melody.

'That sounded lovely,' she commented when the singer ended the piece with a flourish on the strings of his instrument. 'What was it about?'

'It suggests we are lovers,' Rafel told her, his dark eyes sparkling as he discreetly handed the player a generous tip. 'And we will remain so all our lives,' he continued to translate softly, his eyes lingering on her face.

The romantic atmosphere was made complete by the arrival of a flower seller. Rafel took a red carnation, passing it to her with a smile. And as the evening progressed, the alarming events of the past few days faded from her mind. But when eventually she glanced at her watch she knew their precious moments together must come to an end.

'Perhaps I should be getting back to the station,' she suggested. 'I don't like to leave Rosa alone for too long.'

'No,' he protested quickly. 'I will take you. I prefer you do not travel to Castelldefels alone.

And I'd like you to tell me a little more about that fellow, Grey. See if you can get his business address. I want to check it out.'

CHAPTER 6

Fiona was delighted when Rafel rang the following morning. They chatted a while about arrangements to meet, then his voice grew more serious as he continued.

'Fiona, I've been thinking over what you told me about Grey. He's not at all businesslike and I'm inclined to be suspicious.'

'Yes, I agree, but maybe we are worrying unnecessarily. He claims to have been a friend of my late uncle, which could account for his casual attitude to business. In any case, I'm not in a particular hurry to sell . . .'

'I'm very pleased to hear it,' he broke in, and she could sense he was smiling. 'Even so, as Grey didn't leave you his own number, I suggest you call Barcelona, get everything legally settled.'

'I'll give him another hour. If I haven't heard by then, I will do as you suggest, that is, if I can find the number. Ever since my room was ransacked I haven't been able to find the letter I received from Barcelona which was forwarded to me through my mother's solicitor in London.'

'If you can remember the name and address, we can get the number from directory enquiries.'

'No, Rafel, I can't. I believe the name was

99

Roig, or Ruiz, something like that. As for the address, well, Barcelona addresses don't mean a lot to me, but I may be able to contact London.'

'Never mind, I'll ring you in an hour, then we can decide what to do. Should he want to call on you, make sure Rosa is around. And do be careful, darling.'

His term of endearment was music to her ears, and whilst she waited for Grey to make contact she allowed her thoughts to wander back to the previous evening, recalling the warmth of Rafel's embrace before they parted. He had insisted upon driving her home, though she had alighted from the car a short distance from the villa where he waited until she was safely indoors.

The ringing of the telephone in the hall startled her out of her daydream. Her conversation with Grey was brief but satisfactory, and she agreed to meet him in Barcelona the following day.

'By the fountain in Plaça de Cataluña at eleven o'clock,' she confirmed, and repeated his instructions. 'Don't leave the train at Sants, but continue to the next stop. That's fine, so I will see you tomorrow, Mr Grey. I want to get everything dealt with legally, and as soon as possible.'

'Of course, Miss Maxwell,' he agreed, hesitating a moment before he continued casually, 'incidentally, had any more visits from the police?'

A trifle taken aback, she frowned.

'Why do you ask?'

'No special reason. If you remember, the police were going to call on you after the housekeeper had complained about an intruder.'

'Oh, yes, that was the morning you showed me round the area, the day after I arrived.'

'I don't expect the police pursued the matter. They will have other matters to attend to.'

'You're joking,' she said with a short laugh. 'They've never stopped!'

'Really? So what is it that interests them?' he askcd, his tone still casual. 'I would not have thought they'd consider it of such importance.'

'Oh, yes, indeed they do. Well, perhaps I shouldn't say any more. The inspector may not like it.'

'Inspector, eh? So there's a big name on the job.'

'Please, Mr Grey, I'd rather you didn't ask, but before you hang up will you give me the name and telephone number of your firm's main office in Barcelona?'

'Ah yes, I have it here somewhere . . .'

She heard a rustling of paper before he came back to say, 'So sorry, I have a client waiting. I'll give you my business card tomorrow.'

Fiona shrugged. She had felt it unwise to mention something of which the inspector may not approve, but she could not put Rafel's mind at rest regarding her appointment with Herbert Grey.

A short time later, she was delighted when Rafel rang to announce he would be free that morning.

'There's a fiesta in Sitges, or festa, as we call it,' he told her. 'If you would like to experience some local colour, I can pick you up in half an hour.'

*   *   *

Pocketing his car keys Rafel took the telephone receiver off its rest and laid it on the desk, and going to the window he signalled to the man waiting in the unmarked car outside. But when the man made no attempt to move he went to the front door and called, 'Señor! The inspector wishes to speak with you.'

'Inspector Ferrer?' the man queried. 'Ferrer wants me?'

'Si, si, right away!' Rafel said impatiently, indicating the open study door.

With an air of importance, the young officer folded his newspaper and swaggered into the study when without wasting a precious second, Rafel sprinted through the open front door to where his own car was parked beneath the trees.

Thankful the heavy morning traffic had eased, he drove swiftly out of town on a southern route. With luck the officer wouldn't realise he had been deceived until he was well away from the house yet, for a fleeting moment, he felt sympathy for the man knowing he would fall victim to Ferrer's anger.

*   *   *

And Rafel was so right! Ferrer was convinced his blood pressure had risen to an unhealthy limit. He'd had palpitations ever since his fool of an officer had called him from his car outside the Pujol home ten minutes ago to report the professor had managed to leave the house without his knowledge.

'His car has gone. He must have left when you rang for me,' the young officer had admitted nervously, 'but as the line was dead I thought you had been cut off. So, presuming you would call again, I waited by the phone. Had I known, I would have called back immediately.'

'Damned fool!' Ferrer had thundered in response. 'I haven't telephoned the Pujol household today!'

He smacked the desk with his fist, convinced Rafel Pujol would already be on his way to Castelldefels. Yet, thirty minutes later there was still no confirmation of his suspicions. The officer on duty a short distance

103

from the Vancells' villa had not seen a single car pass by.

Ferrer began to feel uneasy. He drew the telephone towards him. He would contact the instrument maker to enquire if he were well enough to receive him. He was, and Ferrer was soon on his way to the village where he lived.

The bruising on Sesrovires' head had faded considerably, Ferrer noticed when he arrived at his workshop. At first the craftsman was a trifle apprehensive, but once he discovered the reason for the inspector's call he gave his visitor a most ingratiating smile.

'I agree entirely,' he said when the subject of the broken guitar came into conversation. 'No-one with any knowledge of its value would have caused such needless damage. Fortunately, it wasn't in the workshop when those men broke in.'

Ferrer's bushy brows rose.

'You still have it?'

'Si, it is here now, but when those men called it was in the cellar of the house—the safest place whilst I waited for the glue to dry.'

'The professor will be pleased,' Ferrer grunted, 'though I'm at a loss to know why.'

The craftsman's expression brightened.

'Ah, si, should you see the professor, will you be kind enough to ask him to call? There is something about this instrument which I find most odd. Well, three things, actually, and I think he will be interested to see.'

104

'And what are they, may I enquire?' Ferrer asked pleasantly. 'I, also, have become quite interested in this particular instrument.'

Sesrovires looked thoughtful for a moment, then began.

'It is very curious, I don't know what to make of it. You see, someone else has worked on this guitar, though for what reason I'm at a loss to understand.'

'Exactly what are you trying to tell me?' Ferrer pressed, his interest increasing. 'Who has worked on it?'

'That I don't know, but someone has removed three of the mother-of-pearl insets on the neck, gouged out a bit more wood, and placed something that looks like pieces of glass behind them before they were reset. They never left this workshop in that state, I do know,' he said as he reached to the bench behind him to bring over the small objects for the inspector's examination. 'I wonder why they bothered.'

Ferrer's eyes widened as he gazed down on the instrument maker's outstretched palm.

'Good gracious!' he breathed in shocked amazement as he scratched glue from one of the pea-sized objects. 'Show me exactly where you found them!'

'Right here, under the inlay,' Sesrovires pointed out. 'I haven't yet replaced the pearl as I thought the professor would like to see this for himself.'

'Diamonds!' Ferrer gasped, barely recovered from his surprise. 'Now I know why they were so keen to get their hands on it!'

Sesrovires gaped.

'Diamonds? In a guitar! But why?'

'That is exactly what I intend to find out!' Ferrer declared, recovering quickly. 'And not a word about this to anyone, understand?'

'Si, si, Inspector, but I must speak with the professor because this guitar had not been re-strung.'

'I'm not skilled in these matters,' Ferrer broke in, 'so I am relying upon you to explain to me every detail.'

*   *   *

Rafel smiled to himself from his position in the station car park. Only seconds after his arrival he'd seen a police car draw up a short distance from the turning to the villa, and observed the change of passengers before it pulled away, tactics which told him Ferrer had the villa under twenty-four hour surveillance.

He was comforted by this knowledge and kept his eyes on the villa, watching for Fiona. When he eventually saw her hurrying towards him, her blue dress accentuating her shapely figure and the sun glinting on her hair, he experienced a familiar surge of pleasure. He'd kept the engine ticking over, and gave a low, appreciative whistle through the open window as she drew alongside, and catching her instant smile he quickly reached over to open the door.

'Let's get moving before anyone notices us,' he said, giving her hand a welcoming squeeze. 'I had hoped to visit Sesrovires but I understand from his wife he's not well enough. Perhaps tomorrow. However, there will be plenty happening in Sitges today.'

I'd like to know more about the culture of this nation,' she said. 'I've read various books.'

'Well, one thing's for sure, no book can tell you what is in my thoughts right now!' he declared, casting her a mischievous sideways glance.

She pouted evocatively and sighed, 'Then how will I ever learn?'

He grinned.

'We'll discuss it one day when we visit my country house. You'll like it, I'm sure. There's a good supply of wine, and the scenery is quite spectacular.'

They continued the journey in this light vein, travelling over the stretch of road, which wound along the cliff face overlooking the sea, to reach the busy little town of Sitges. Today, the place was ablaze with colour, and it seemed that every child in the town had donned traditional costume to join a parade that wound its way through the narrow streets. There were boys carrying fireworks, followed by stick dancers who paused to perform their traditional ritual on every corner. Pretty, dark-eyed girls shook tambourines as they practised their intricate steps on the cobbled surface, and another child, encased in the mould of a papier-mâché dragon which belched fire and smoke from its nostrils, trudged along behind.

When this colourful parade reached the town square, young Castellers sprang barefoot on to the shoulders of others in a tower that trembled precariously. But, Rafel told her, it was no less serious a competition than that of their fathers who, when evening came, would climb to make a pyramid of six or seven tiers. Fiona was fascinated.

As the festivities continued, her eyes wandered over the onlookers lining the square. Mothers and fathers cheered their offspring, whilst grandmothers contentedly fluttered their fans as they looked on from the shade of the doorway.

Rafel watched Fiona's changing expressions as she followed the celebrations with interest.

'Tonight they will dance sardanas in this square,' he told her. 'Perhaps you would care to try.'

'I'd love to,' she agreed, her eyes shining in anticipation, 'though you'll have to be patient with me. I've never done anything like it before.'

He smiled.

'This is one tradition which has been kept alive, when the musicians continue to play age-old tunes. You will enjoy it, I'm sure, and even without the traditional shoes, you should quickly learn the steps. Very shortly the crowd will disperse for lunch so we may as well do likewise as there will be little to see until the early evening.'

After a leisurely meal and a rest in the leafy gardens of the hotel where they had dined on their previous visit, Rafel took her hand and they strolled down towards the sea. Deep in conversation, they walked along the shore, barely aware of the distance they had covered until they turned back to go in the direction of the church which stood in an elevated position at the end of the promenade.

'You're so wonderful to be with, I lose all sense of time,' Rafel said, sliding his arm round her waist.

'Mm, it's gone so quickly,' she agreed, resting her head against his shoulder, 'but it's been a really lovely day.'

He smiled down on her. 'It is not over yet, Fiona. There's still the dancing to come, but we can enjoy a drink until the music begins.'

Seated in cane chairs outside a bar, she watched whilst the musicians positioned their music stands and instruments on the stage which had been erected earlier in the day. Soon more people were beginning to congregate around it, young and old, all waiting for the music to start. She felt Rafel's hand reach for hers where it rested on the arm of her chair and she turned to meet his steady gaze.

'You will have to tell me what steps to do,' she said a trifle unsteadily when his eyes lingered upon her. 'I don't want to make a fool of myself.'

'You won't,' he assured her. 'I think the music is about to play so finish your drink and we'll go over to the promenade to practise a few steps. It's growing dark so no-one will notice.'

As they crossed to the promenade the music began, a reedy sound like that of an oboe, another like a flute, playing a tune with a curiously different rhythm.

'I can't imagine a dance to accompany such music,' she commented as he drew her into the shadow of a palm tree, 'though I recall you promising to teach me so that we could join in the dancing in Barcelona.'

'You shall have that lesson now, then you will be ready to join in outside the cathedral one Sunday at noon.'

'Do you think we ever will?' she asked with a doubtful sigh. 'It seems like this business with the police will never end.'

'Of course it will, darling, and now we are together let us enjoy the dancing.'

She returned his smile and took his outstretched hand when, for a few moments, they stood side by side whilst he counted aloud to the tempo.

'At first we keep our joined hands down by our sides,' he instructed as the music continued its curious rhythm. 'Now, left forward, one, two, three, right forward, one two, three, left . . . that's it, keep going.'

They continued practising these steps until the music stopped. Now she listened for a beat on the little drum followed by a few bars played on a whistle, then stepped forward and back the way he had instructed as the other instruments joined in. Back and forth, back and forth to the strange rhythm until she found herself relaxing when the steps became easier to follow.

'Rafel, this is fun'!' she exclaimed laughingly. 'Am I doing all right?'

'Si, but now more quickly,' he directed as the beat speeded up, 'and we raise our hands. You are doing well.'

He smiled encouragingly then, as the rhythm changed once more, said, 'Quickly now, left, left, left, right, right, right, left, two three—wonderful!'

When the dance ended she was quite out of breath and he caught her up in his arms.

'Try to imagine a big circle of people, and maybe a smaller one in the centre, all hand in hand, young and old, dancing these steps. That is the sardana, a tradition which lives on in Cataluña,' he ended with a kiss.

'You're a very good teacher,' she said a trifle breathlessly. 'Can we try it again?'

'Yes, but now I think you are competent enough to join the others,' he decided, leading her to an area nearer the church where the street lamps illuminated the waiting circle of dancers.

When the little drum gave the signal to start, they joined the circle, Rafel quietly reminding her of the steps once the music began.

* * *

With a groan of discomfort, Ferrer reached into his desk drawer for two more indigestion tablets. Tied to the office, awaiting information, there had been no opportunity to go home and enjoy his wife's superb cooking, no time for a sesta, and still Pujol had not returned to his home. Reaching for the internal phone, he snapped out an order.

'Double the watch on both Vancells' villa and Pujol's home. No-one is to be apprehended at this stage, but report all movements to me. And, should Pujol return, I want to know, immediately!'

* * *

It was quite late when they left the fiesta. Fiona had enjoyed the dancing and felt confident she could repeat the steps outside the cathedral one Sunday morning. And now, still exhilarated from the spectacular display of fireworks that had followed, she relaxed as Rafel drove her home.

'Unfortunately, I have to give a lecture in the morning,' he said, 'otherwise I would have met you at the station, or come for you in the car.'

'Don't forget, you're supposed to keep away from Castelldefels,' she reminded him. 'In any case, it shouldn't prove difficult to find the place to meet Grey and I don't want to upset the inspector if I can avoid it.'

'You may be right. Not that I wish to interfere in your private affairs,' he added hurriedly. 'I'm merely concerned for your safey.'

'I'll be careful, Rafel, I promise. Anyway, if I'm to live in this area, it will do me good to find my way around the city.'

'True,' he agreed with a smile. 'Perhaps one day you will come to my home. I know my mother will be delighted to meet you, and you can take a look at my collection of old instruments.'

'If I do, will you play for me? I love the sound of classic guitar.'

'If you wish,' he said, and continued eagerly, 'Why not tomorrow? We'll meet at two, as arranged, have lunch in the city, then I'll take you to my home.'

'I'd like that, Rafel,' she said, then giggled as she added, 'but just imagine Inspector

113

Ferrer's expression if he should see us together!'

CHAPTER 7

Fiona had only a short wait for the train that would take her into the centre of Barcelona. She had studied the street map Rafel had given her the previous evening and, once there, followed the directions to Plaça de Catalunya. It was a warm, sunny day, and she had chosen to wear a cream silk dress with sleeves, knowing it would be suitable for both her business appointment with Mr Grey and her visit to Rafel's home.

She spotted Herbert Grey leaning against a huge, modern sculpture in the busy square, the jacket of his dark suit over his arm. He was speaking into a mobile phone until he caught sight of her when he quickly returned it to his pocket and headed her way. It reminded her to check for her own mobile and she felt for it through the soft linen of her bag. At two o'clock she would ring Rafel to tell him exactly where she was.

'Good morning, Miss Maxwell,' Grey said smoothly. 'Did you experience any trouble getting here?'

'No. I'd just missed one train but found my way quite easily once I arrived. Hope I haven't kept you waiting.'

He shrugged and dabbed perspiration from his forehead as he enquired, 'Not too hot for you, is it?'

'Thanks, I'm fine, but what a busy place,' she remarked as they paused at a pedestrian crossing where a constant stream of traffic passed by. 'Do you enjoy working here?'

'It has its moments,' he replied as the lights changed and they crossed towards a towering department store.

'Where exactly are we going?' she asked, walking briskly to keep up with him. 'Is your office very far away?'

'No, not far, but because it is being redecorated, I'm sharing an office with a friend of mine. I'm afraid it's rather small, but its serves my purpose.'

'What about the main branch? Are you not able to work from there?' she queried as they left the busy square.

'Too far out of the city,' he said. 'Bad for business.'

She gave a nod of understanding. Farther along, they turned left, passing the restaurant where she had dined with Rafel, to continue into narrowing, dark streets when she began to wonder how anyone seeking his services would know where to find him.

'Almost there,' he told her, 'then we'll soon have things sorted out.'

'But how one earth does anyone know where to find you?'

He grinned and drew the mobile from his pocket.

'They use this number, Miss Maxwell, you see.'

'Ah, yes, I must take a note of your number, also the name of your firm.'

'All in good time,' he said, pausing before a drab-looking door. 'First, let us go inside and discuss this property of yours.'

Once inside, Grey indicated she should take a seat on one of the gaudy plastic chairs that were set before a shabby desk. The ashtray on it was overflowing and the air heavy with the smell of stale cigarette smoke. A younger man came through a door at the back of the makeshift office, bringing with him a draught of air that sent the few papers in the open file fluttering to the floor.

'I will get them,' he said in English when she attempted to pick them up.

'Juan is my partner,' Grey told her. 'It helps to have a local man, particularly when it comes to understanding the local laws.'

'Yes, I expect it will,' she replied, becoming a trifle uneasy under the younger man's intense stare. 'Is there a lot of work involved in transferring the deeds of the villa? I'd like to get it done as soon as possible.'

Grey's smile didn't reach his eyes as he took a seat opposite.

'Come now, Miss Maxwell, there's no need to make a hasty decision. You have to be sure you could settle here. Your uncle used to tell me about your comfortable home in Sussex, how you loved it there.'

'Actually, it's Surrey,' she corrected him with a suspicious frown. 'But I'd only moved down from Edinburgh a few weeks before so I didn't have the opportunity to let my uncle know. In fact, the solicitors' letter informing me of his death went to my Edinburgh address. It was redirected, of course, but I was away when it finally arrived which is the reason I was unable to attend his funeral.'

'Surrey, of course, how silly of me. Even so, it's a big wrench, you know. Think of all your friends and neighbours. They would miss you terribly.'

She was beginning to be annoyed by his patronising manner, and replied coolly, 'As I said, I wasn't there long enough to make friends, or get to know the neighbours, so there's no point in you trying to persuade me to return.'

His mouth widened in a mirthless smile.

'Quite the little madam, aren't you?' he began until Juan broke in with a few words of rapid Spanish whereupon Grey reverted to his previous manner.

'Actually, my dear, we'd like to make you an offer,' he said and paused to note her reaction. 'You hand over the guitar and, in exchange for this little favour, we will ensure your housekeeper comes to no harm.'

For a moment she was stunned.

'You will what?' she managed to gasp.

118

'We know you have it, so if you want to save her any pain, I suggest you do as I say.'

'Now I understand what you're up to and why you want me out of the way,' she said, endeavouring to keep her head, 'but what makes you think the guitar is with me?'

Grey gave a triumphant snort as he replied. 'We know it wasn't in Pujol's car when he returned to Barcelona after visiting Sesrovires, and neither was it in the repairer's workshop, so it doesn't require too much intelligence to now he must have left it with you!'

'An do you imagine I will hand it over without question?' she asked, managing to keep an even voice.

'Yes, I do!' Grey hissed. 'And this time don't involve the police or you will discover there's been a fire in a certain villa in Castelldefels.'

'You wouldn't dare!' she broke in with a surge of courage. 'You profess to have been a friend of my uncle, yet you'd do a despicable thing like that! You're the last person I'd consider to be his friend.'

'Shut up, woman!' Grey snarled, and, turning to the other man, directed, 'Show her the letter, Juan. We'll soon see what little Miss Know-all Maxwell has to say to that.'

'All I want to see are the deeds to my house!' she retorted as the young man placed a printed sheet of paper on the table.

As he pushed it towards her, she had to make a supreme effort to suppress any outward sign of fear when she saw half of the index finger on his left hand was missing!

'Not deeds exactly,' Grey was saying, 'but I believe you've seen a copy of this before, right?'

Struggling to focus on the words in front of her, she nodded, recognising the list of names was an exact copy of the one she possessed— names of the students of Jaume's father, like the one her uncle had supplied. Only this time she found Rafel's name was highlighted in yellow and beside it a hand-written note which read, '*Remember, I was at the sale, and it was the same guitar Jaume Vancells claimed to have had stolen from him in Brussels. As I said in my fax, the name highlighted was the buyer, not the niece, so this time don't botch the job. Get it back and find the gems. It's a valuable instrument, or so Jaume Vancells once told me. I'll be back for my share!*' And it was signed, Frank.

'Well?' Grey prompted with a cruel twist of his lips. 'Now you can appreciate why we need to have the instrument in our possession.'

Fiona's mind was in turmoil. To protect Rosa, she had to agree, but could she bluff it out, promise to produce the guitar without letting them know it was still with the repairer? Aware it must have been Grey who was behind the scheme to confiscate the guitar in the first place, she faced up to him with a lift of her chin.

'But I thought it had already been in your possession!'

'Oh, yes, it has, but when we get hold of it this time we'll do the job properly, chop the thing into little pieces if necessary. Now we know what we're looking for is not an item of any great size.'

Used to coping in a crisis, Fiona stalled for time. Somehow she had to get word to Rafel, but he would be giving his lecture, which wouldn't finish until one. She took a surreptitious glance at her watch and saw it had just turned noon, then looked up to see the expectant smirk on Grey's face and knew she had to make a decision.

'Well, I suppose you give me no alternative but to hand it over,' she said with a shrug of submission. 'Though by the time I catch a train to Castelldefels, it will be a while before I get it back here.'

'My dear Miss Maxwell,' Grey began, oozing charm, 'I wouldn't dream of putting you to all that trouble. I shall drive you to Castelldefels in my car.'

'How very kind,' she said, and her mind was working quickly as she continued, 'I must first make sure Rosa is at home as I haven't brought a key. I'm sure there will be a telephone kiosk nearby.'

'No need, use this,' Grey said, handing over his mobile phone.

Fiona had memorised Rafel's number and,

much as she hated to disturb him during lectures, there was a no real alternative. Holding the instrument close to her ear, she soon heard his brisk reply.

'Rosa, it's me,' she began in a clear voice, and continued quickly, 'I'm glad I caught you, as Mr Grey is driving me over to the villa to collect the guitar. Have it ready, will you? Yes, I know you're going out at two,' she rushed on, to mask the sound of Rafel's voice, 'so if it is not convenient, let me know. Just a moment, I'll give you my number . . .'

'Oh no, you won't!' Grey hissed, snatching the mobile from her hand.

'She merely asked where I am so that she can let me know when she's leaving!' Fiona snapped. 'I can't expect her to wait around all day!'

'She is your servant,' Juan remarked. 'She should do as you ask without question.'

'Rosa has been a loyal servant for years. I'm not going to repay her by treating her like a slave!' she shot back, rising to her feet.

'Enough of your sentiments! Sit down!' Grey snarled, and turning to Juan directed, 'Bring the car, will you? I don't intend to waste any more time arguing here!'

*   *   *

Rafel returned to his students with an apologetic shrug.

'I'm afraid this session will have to be cut short. My presence is urgently required elsewhere. If you will write down your questions and hand them to my assistant, I'll reply to them during our next session,' he informed the group and hurried from the room to consider what action he should take.

Fiona had given the impression of being quite calm, though he sensed a certain tension her voice. But why say she was going to the villa to collect the guitar when she knew it was in Sesrovires workshop? Should it be merely a ruse to protect the instrument maker, then she was taking a great risk. By what she said, Grey was with her, otherwise she would have answered when he asked where she was speaking from rather than continue to chatter on and on. He had no facility to recall the number, no way of knowing her present position. He never had trusted this man, Grey from the start and now, as he hurried into his office, he knew only one course was left to him. He must get in touch with Ferrer.

Cursing the guitar under his breath, he waited to hear the inspector's voice. He should have insisted he go with her. She was far too trusting and vulnerable . . .

*   *   *

When Juan left to pick up the car, Grey got to his feet and went to peer through the glass panel in the door. There were people passing in the street outside, but Fiona knew she had little chance of attracting anyone's attention before Grey was alerted to her intention to escape.

There was absolutely no chance of using her mobile while he was around, and nothing at hand she could strike him with to do enough damage whilst she got away. Her thoughts went to the contents of her bag. Nothing sharp in there, but the hair spray she carried could temporarily dissable him if she could manage to take careful aim.

Casually sliding her hand into the bag, she withdrew a handkerchief. Catching his suspicious glance, she merely dabbed her nose and returned it, taking a grip on the small canister of hairspray as she did so. Easing off the top under cover of the bag, she moved casually towards the door, to look out on the street.

'Does he have far to go?' she asked, her finger ready on the nozzle.

Grey compressed his lips and shrugged, his brows raised as he turned to speak when she aimed for his eyes with the full force of the stinging spray.

'What the hell!' he yelled as his hands flew to his face. 'You little bitch!'

She didn't hesitate, grabbing for the door handle as he continued to curse, and it was only when she reached the street that she became aware of the mobile ringing in her bag.

* * *

The inspector gave a satisfied grunt, the pains in his stomach fading as Rafel related the details of Fiona's call.

'At last, we are getting somewhere!' he exclaimed, and went on to insist Rafel should stay where he was. 'If necessary, I'll go to Castelldefels, though my officer here tells me the housekeeper has had no calls from Miss Maxwell.'

'But, Inspector, why would she say the guitar is at the villa when it is still with Sesrovires?'

'I have not had the opportunity to tell you until now—I have it.'

'You have it?' Rafel echoed. 'Why is that? I hope Sesrovires is not in danger.'

'No, no, in fact he asked me to tell you, and if you would care to come alone to the station I'll discuss it with you.'

'Right now, I'm more concerned about Miss Maxwell. She hasn't answered my call. I must know where she is.'

'Keep your phone switched on. She may call you again, and give me the number in case I need to reach you,' Ferrer directed, and reminded him, 'At least you have called us. Obviously, this is what she hoped you would do.'

Rafel had left the music department at speed to travel to the inspector's office. He supposed Ferrer was right. In a difficult situation, Rosa must have been the only name she could use without arousing suspicion. And following a brief discussion with the inspector, he now knew why he was holding the guitar at the station.

'So, if they didn't find it when they visited Sesrovires, they are bound to think it is either at the villa or with you, professor,' Ferrer concluded.

'Yet it doesn't explain how they missed the stones in the first place,' Rafel put in, 'unless they had no idea what they were looking for.'

'But now I suspect they do, though from what source I can't say, unless the Señorita knew more than we realised and was pressed into revealing this information.'

Rafel glanced up in horror.

'Do you mean threatened in some way?'

'It depends if she was aware of Jaume's hidden treasures. For some time, we'd treated his trips to Brussels with suspicion, but just when we hoped to apprehend him, the guitar was conveniently stolen.'

'Look here, Inspector, I'm sure she didn't know anything about the diamonds.'

'Calm yourself, Professor. Keep a clear head in case you get another call. I'm wanted in the lab but I suggest you remain here then, should we receive news of Miss Maxwell, you will be one of the first to know.'

*   *   *

Fiona dashed along the street, sometimes bumping into anyone who happened to be in her path, regardless of their furious stares. She had no idea in which direction she was going and cut through narrow alleyways and squares in her desperate need to get away from Grey. She didn't know how long it would take him to recover and give chase, but felt it safer to seek out busy public areas in preference to deserted streets.

Her need to contact Rafel brought her to a breathless halt in a wide doorway. She could tell this was the old quarter by the height and design of the buildings she had passed. But there was no sign to inform her of the location, only a high stone wall loomed along one side of a pedestrian area, and the strangest cry came from somewhere beyond it, like that of a flock of geese.

Struggling to recover her breath, she entered Rafel's number and heard him reply surprisingly quickly.

'Fiona! Are you all right? Where are you, darling?'

The relief of hearing his voice was too much to bear and her throat constricted with unshed tears so that she could hardly speak.

'Oh, Rafel,' she managed to gasp, 'I don't

127

know—I'm lost!'

'You're not with Grey?'

'I got away,' she told him brokenly. 'He was really horrible.'

'He hasn't hurt you, has he?' he responded quickly.

She shook her head, but before she could assure him, he broke in to say, 'Tell me, Fiona, are you still in the city?'

'Yes, but I don't know where, I just ran.'

'Look around you . . . the buildings. Any traffic?'

She took a gulp of air and steadied herself to reply, 'I can hear cars, at the end of the street, I think, and the buildings are old . . .'

'What's that noise?' he interrupted as again there came that raucous cry from somewhere beyond the wall.

'I don't know—sounds like geese.'

'Geese!' he exclaimed. 'So you could be in the park, or near the zoo. Is there anything else you can see?'

'The street is narrow. There's a high building at one side, and near Grey's office I saw the Snails restaurant, but I ran in the opposite direction to get away.'

'Fiona, you're in the Gothic quarter. It's the geese in the cathedral cloisters you can hear! Now, go into the building, mingle with the crowd. I'll leave a message for Ferrer and be with you as quickly as I can.'

The relief of hearing Rafel's voice had left

her feeling drained, but she knew she had to enter the cathedral as he instructed, to reach the safety of the crowd. Continuing along the narrow, paved street she became aware of the sound of music, rather like that she had heard in Sitges during the week. The sound continued to grow louder when, much to her surprise, she suddenly found herself in the crowded area in front of the main doors of the cathedral. The music came from the band of musicians accompanying a large circle of people preparing to dance a sardana. Hesitating a moment, she listened and looked around as the reedy notes of the musicians continued to play and the dancers began their steady rhythm.

From which direction would Rafel arrive, she wondered and scanned the watching crowd until, to her horror, across the square she spotted the sandy-haired figure of Herbert Grey climbing the steps, with Juan beside him. When Juan looked up, she drew back into the crowd, looking wildly around in search of Rafel until mounting fear impelled her to join the circle of dancers. This was one place where it was unlikely she'd be noticed.

An inner ring had formed inside the larger one, and she quickly ducked under the arms of the outer circle to join with the one inside. Flinging her bag into the centre amongst others already piled there, she broke into the circle of dancers, putting them temporarily out of step.

Somehow, though trembling and breathless, she managed to keep the rhythm, counting silently, one, two, three, one, two, three, just as Rafel had done, concentrating on the steps in case she caused those next to her to drop out. She could see Grey shading his eyes from the bright sun as he scanned the crowd, whilst Juan searched the opposite direction.

The music played on, but the tension within made her falter in her step. She gave the man next to her an apologetic glance, but he smiled encouragingly and tightened his grip, lifting her hand high as the little drum was struck, the whistle played, and the tempo quickened.

The pace quickened again as they came to the third phase of the dance. She concentrated hard, suddenly horrified when she felt the grip on her right hand loosen, and her heart lurched as she cast a sideways glance to see Rafel.

'Keep dancing,' he whispered, closing his warm fingers firmly around hers, and he prayed silently that the officer at the station had appreciated the urgency of his message.

'I'm so glad you're here,' she gasped, struggling to keep in step.

He saw her face was ashen and sensed she was about to succumb to her weariness.

'Don't give up yet,' he urged. 'Ferrer's on his way.'

'That's Grey and his accomplice,' she said,

nodding in the direction of the steps.

'Grey's the one with fair hair?'

'Yes, the other one is Juan.'

'But who is the younger man with them?' Rafel asked, his tone urgent. 'He's very like the one I saw at the sale in London and, I suspect, he is the last student your uncle tutored.'

'Rose would know,' she put in quickly. 'She saw him at the funeral, talking to Grey. He could be Frank, the one who wrote the note.'

'I believe I know him, too, at least, by reputation.'

'What do you think they'll do?' she asked worriedly. 'Grey threatened to harm Rosa, set fire to the villa.'

'When the music stops, simply walk away. Don't worry, Ferrer and his men will be close behind,' he assured her, catching her nervous glance.

'How can you be sure?'

'Because I've just seen Ferrer come up the steps, and he's already spotted us.'

As the music stopped and the applause faded, Fiona grabbed his arm.

'Don't leave me, will you?' she pleaded, her violet eyes glistening with tears.

'Of course not. I'll be right behind you, but not too close. Let them think you're on your own.

*   *   *

131

As the crowd began to disperse, Fiona picked up her bag and strolled away. About to enter a narrow street lined with shops, she paused to take a surreptitious glance at the reflection in a shop window and saw that Grey and Juan were following. Confident the inspector would also be close behind, she decided to continue along the street, hesitating a moment to avoid colliding with someone directly in front. But fear gripped her when she glanced up to discover it was the tall, young man last seen standing beside Grey and Juan.

'What's the hurry, Miss Maxwell?' he said, smirking.

'So, you know who I am,' she declared once she had recovered from his unexpected presence, 'and I believe I'm correct in assuming you are Frank.'

'Think you're clever, don't you,' he sneered, 'but you won't escape me so easily.'

Suddenly aware of another man looking in the shop window beside them, she glanced anxiously round to find Grey and Juan closing in and felt increasingly vulnerable. But the action following was carried out with such speed and efficiency, she wouldn't have believed it possible.

She saw the man who had been gazing in the shop window move quickly forward to pin Frank's arms behind his back. Then, from behind, came sounds of a scuffle. She heard

Rafel call her name and he pulled her aside in time to see Herbert Grey and his accomplice being removed by the police.

'It's over, darling,' Rafel whispered, cradling her head against his chest. 'You're quite safe.'

'I was beginning to feel extremely nervous,' she admitted, her arms sliding round his waist.

As they clung together, Ferrer came to a breathless halt beside them.

'Thank God you stayed with the dancers,' he said. 'It gave me time to gather my men together. We were able to observe their every move.'

'I was beginning to wonder if you'd got my message,' Rafel admitted. 'Goodness knows what would have happened, otherwise.'

'Once you knew where the Señorita was you should have waited for me at the station,' Ferrer reprimanded him. 'It was more serious than you realised.'

'More serious, Inspector!' Rafel exclaimed. 'After what Fiona has suffered, also Sesrovires and old Rosa, plus the threat to the villa . . .'

'Also what happened to you at the airport?' Fiona interjected. 'That injection could have killed you.'

'Plus the damage to your increasingly valuable guitar,' Ferrer reminded him with a surreptitious smile. 'Unless I can prove the gems were being smuggled, you may be a very rich man!'

Fiona looked horrified.

'Does this mean my uncle was a smuggler?'

The inspector stroked his fleshy chin.

'Difficult to say, Señorita, but even if we prove anything, you will not be held responsible. Incidentally, we found the letter you mentioned on one of the men, and I noticed Grey's accomplice had only part of one finger, proof that he was the one at the villa the day after you arrived.'

She sighed and declared, 'But, concerning the villa, I still don't have legal proof of ownership.'

'Ah, yes, this reminds me,' Ferrer broke in. 'We also discovered another letter addressed to you which had been sent to London from a firm of solicitors in Barcelona. I will let you have it before you return to England, if that is your intention?'

'I certainly hope not,' Rafel intervened. 'I would prefer Miss Maxwell to remain here.'

Fiona glanced up at him to say, 'I would like to, but my belongings are in England.'

'Surely they can be moved?'

'Yes, but I have no employment here.'

Rafel laughed and drew her close to suggest softly, 'Then, let us be married.'

'Married!' she echoed in surprise.

Ferrer's brows rose and he signalled to one of his men.

'Because I love you, so why not?' Rafel asked, lifting her chin so that she looked directly into his eyes. 'Do you love me enough?'

'Mm, very much,' she murmured as his lips came down to capture hers in a lingering kiss.

'Congratulations, Professor, I won't trouble you further just now,' Rafel heard the inspector say.

From the corner of his eye he watched Ferrer stroll away, and saw the broad smile on his face when he turned and raised his hand before getting into the waiting car to disappear in the continuous swirl of traffic, leaving Fiona and Rafel hand in hand, safe at last.